P9-DNZ-693

Kelly and Me

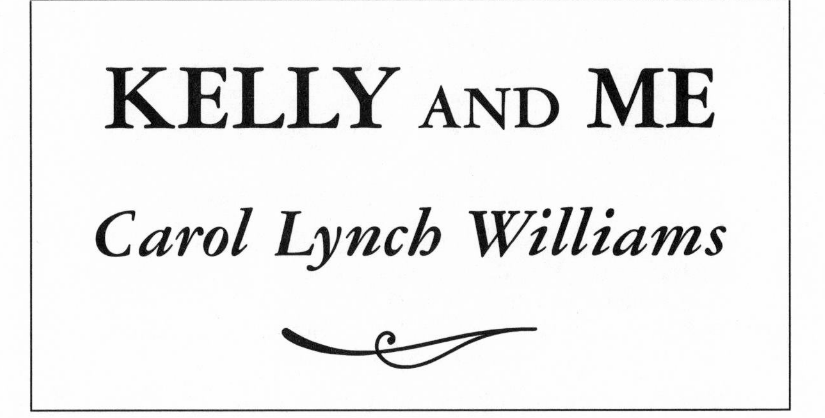
KELLY AND ME
Carol Lynch Williams

Delacorte
Press

To Drew and Samantha and Papa

Published by
Delacorte Press
Bantam Doubleday Dell Publishing Group, Inc.
1540 Broadway
New York, New York 10036

Library of Congress Cataloging in Publication Data

Williams, Carol Lynch.
Kelly and me / by Carol Lynch Williams.
p. cm.
Summary: Eleven-year-old Leah has a summer of outrageous adventures in her small Florida community, some involving her freethinking grandfather but all shared with her younger sister, Kelly, until an unexpected loss changes their lives.
ISBN 0-385-30897-3
[1. Sisters—Fiction. 2. Family life—Fiction. 3. Grandfathers—Fiction. 4. Death—Fiction. 5. Florida—Fiction.] I. Title.
PZ7.W65588Ke 1993
[Fic]—dc20 92-20492
CIP
AC

Design by Diane Stevenson/SNAP • HAUS GRAPHICS

Manufactured in the United States of America

October 1993

10 9 8 7 6 5 4 3 2 1

BVG

May

THE WRECK

Kelly and I were barely out of school for summer vacation when Momma and Daddy finally tried locking Papa into his room. Papa is our grampa and he's been staying with us since Grammy died a couple of years ago.

Anyway. It was only ten in the morning and Papa was on another one of his drinking sprees. He doesn't always drink a lot, only when he feels troubled, or when he starts remembering, and I guess he was remembering some pretty sad things, because Momma was starting to get worried. I don't know why. Papa is always a lot of fun when he's had a little to drink. Except when it gets dark. Then at night, because our bedroom is next to his, I can hear him crying and whispering names.

Well, Kelly and I were peeking around a corner watching Daddy try to maneuver Papa into my old room.

When Papa came to live with us, we drew straws to see whose room Papa would take, since there are only three bedrooms in our house. I lost, but it's not too bad sharing a room with Kelly. She's neat, and if I leave my bed unmade, she'll sometimes make it for me.

"This old coot is as strong as an ox," Daddy said. He was sweating pretty bad and his face was really red. It nearly matched the color of his hair. He had Papa in one of those championship wrestling moves you see on TV, and if Momma hadn't been so worried, I would have suggested he change careers and be a wrestler. He would have been pretty good, too, except for the sweat.

"I'll show you strong," said Papa. He was trying to whip around and get Daddy in a half nelson. Maybe *he* should come out of retirement and be a professional wrestler.

"Just don't hurt him, Andy," Momma said. Now, if you ask me, Kelly looks just like Momma. I bet when she's all grown up, Kelly will look the way Momma does now: tall and thin, light hair turned a shade or two darker. Freckles still. I think my mother is beautiful. I tend to take after Daddy. I'm a little short for my age, and in the sun my hair shines red highlights. Momma says I'll be glad about that when I'm older. I don't know.

"Yeah, Daddy. Please don't hurt Papa," Kelly said. She was almost crying. Kelly has a real soft heart. She hardly ever watches professional wrestling with me and Papa. She thinks it's not very ladylike, and I guess she's right, but I bug her anyway and tell her my wildest dream is to be partners with her in a sisters tag team. We could be called the Snortin' Ortons, but she won't even think about it.

"What about me?" Daddy shouted, pushing Papa into the bedroom. He closed and locked the door, then fell against it, breathing heavily. He left a sweat mark on the dark oak. Papa started beating on the door. There was a lump in my throat, and I just couldn't figure out why. I hated to see Papa locked up, but Momma was sure he was going to hurt himself with all his drinking.

"I fought in a war," he shouted, "so we could all be free and you lock me in here. The Koreans were better to me than you are."

Momma looked like she felt a little guilty, but relieved, and we all went downstairs so Papa could have a chance to get some sleep.

Papa was never more than a social drinker when Grammy was alive. When she started losing her health, she and Papa decided the best place to live was where there was someone who could help look after her. At the Pink Flamingo Retirement Home, Grammy and Papa had their own apartment and everything. It seems like they were barely settled in when we were all called to tell her good-bye.

I can remember it like it was yesterday. It still makes me sad to think about Grammy, her being gone and all. Papa is sad too. He doesn't ever say it, but I can tell. And when the memories get too heavy for him, he'll drink.

Kelly and I went downstairs for lunch and to wait for Papa to take a nap. People are always saying that it's easy to see Kelly and I are from the same family. Sometimes we're mistaken for twins, I guess because we're nearly the same height. And we both have blond hair, although Kelly is almost a towhead. Her eyes are real green, like Momma's, and my eyes are light blue, like Daddy's. And then, we're real close in age. I'm eleven and Kelly is ten.

We had our bathing suits on under our clothes, just in case. See, we were supposed to go to the beach with Papa, and if he was feeling okay later on, we still wanted to go. Living in Florida has its advantages. Our house is only five miles from the ocean, so we start each vacation by spending a day at New Smyrna Beach.

After a while the banging and shouting stopped. Momma told Daddy it would be okay to go to the store now, and Kelly and I went out to play. If we hadn't been waiting to see if Papa would be feeling better later, Kelly and I would have ridden our bikes over to our cousin Samantha's house. She lives right near the beach.

It wasn't very long before Kelly saw Papa hanging out the bedroom window. We were in the backyard, under one of the peach trees, pretending the bees were part of our royal court, when she said, "Well, I'll be cat-kicked." That's something Papa is always saying when he's surprised. I looked to where Kelly was staring wide-eyed, and my mouth fell open.

"Ohmyheck," I said, and stood up.

Papa was backing out the second-story window, Spider-Man fashion, and using Momma's good sheets as a rope. Momma was not going to like that at all. We ran over to where he was inching his way down the clapboard and looked up at him. Lots of people say that Papa is pretty darn spry for a seventy-two-year-old man, and I guess that they're right. My best guy friend, Tom Blandford, his grandmother can't get around without a wheelchair. And Shelly Diamond, from school, her grandfather is a lot younger than Papa is and he's starting to go senile.

Papa even looks young. His hair is white, but that's all there is that's old on him. He's kind of short and lean and when he makes a muscle, it's like squeezing iron. He has all of his teeth and his eyes are so green people think he's wearing contact lenses. All the old widowed ladies from church used to come and visit Papa a lot after Grammy died, but he let it be known in no uncertain terms that he was not interested in getting married again. Now the only person who ever comes over that's not related and is old, is Mrs. Comer from next door. But she never comes to visit Papa. They hate each other.

Well, anyway. Papa's shoes were leaving perfect prints on Daddy's freshly painted house. Daddy was not going to like that at all either, seeing he had spent one entire weekend painting. No, Momma and Daddy were not going to like this.

"Go get my dog, Leah," Papa said to me, when he glanced down and saw us staring bug-eyed at him, "and put him in the car. We're going to the beach."

"No way, Papa," I said. "Uh-uh, no way. Momma and Daddy are not going to be very happy about what you're doing."

"Yeah, Papa," Kelly said. "Those are Momma's designer sheets you're using to escape with."

Papa dropped on the ground beside us, landing in a crouch. He just missed landing in the giant hibiscus bush Daddy planted years ago so no one would be able to peek in our downstairs bathroom window. The sheets, striped like a tiger and knotted every foot or so, swung gently against the white house.

"They were the only ones in the room," Papa said. "When I escaped from those Koreans during the war I didn't ask them which sheets I should use." He wiped his hands together, then began to crawl toward the garage, where his old Cadillac was parked. I guess there is something else that's old about Papa. His car. We followed him, walking, till he waved us down with his hand. Then we crouched too. The garage never seemed so far away. It's set back only a hundred feet from the house, but the heat made it seem farther than it was.

"Papa," I said. "You don't have to hide. Momma and Daddy have gone to Wal-Mart."

"I have a feeling that you're going to get in big trouble," Kelly said to Papa. "And us too. And you know my feelings. They are always right."

Papa whistled for George Furd.

"Remember the last time I said we were gonna get in trouble?" Kelly said to me. "Remember? I said that we should *not* watch the whole 'Star Wars' series at Tom's house, and we did, and Momma had an infarction. Remember?"

"I remember," I said.

"I'm always right about my feelings," Kelly said. She was kind of smug. But she *is* always right, so I couldn't argue with her.

George Furd came running up, licked Papa once in the face, then plopped down to rest in the shade Papa's body made. I don't know how Papa can stand that old dog's stinky breath. Even after a deodorant chew biscuit there's hardly a punishment worse than letting George Furd breathe on someone.

It was too hot for too much activity, especially for crouching, so I sat down with the dog. As soon as I did, Papa was off running toward the garage, signaling with one hand and bent over like he was crippled. George Furd walked slowly to the car and jumped into his spot beside Papa. No matter where Papa goes, whether it's only a few blocks to the Red and White grocery store, or if it's all the way to Georgia, George Furd goes too. And he always sits in the front.

Kelly and I climbed into the back of the car. Papa slid down, one knee pointing high beside the steering wheel. He could barely look over the dashboard.

"Lay low," he ordered, and started the car. Only George Furd could be seen. His stiff yellow hair was standing up on end, looking like he had recently gone to the barbershop with Papa and gotten his fur buzzed.

George Furd has one very blue eye and one very brown eye. This makes it hard to know which eye to look at whenever I have heart-to-heart talks with him about his breath. I don't want to hurt his feelings by looking in the wrong eye. Papa says the different-colored eyes come from his ancestors. Papa swears George's mother was a timber wolf and his father was a Kodiak bear. Kelly and I know that's not true, though, because Papa has a tendency to exaggerate.

George Furd's head was hanging out the window, his tongue lolling out the side of his mouth, spit rolling and dripping in the wind. We almost hit the mailbox trying to get out of the yard, but Papa avoided it by driving through the ditch. He then drove down the sidewalk nearly a half block till he had to swerve onto the road so as not to run into Mrs. Comer's mailbox.

"Steer clear of Wal-Mart," I said from the floor of the car. And then we were off.

The first place we stopped was the Red and White. That's the corner mom-and-pop store in our little neighborhood. You can find nearly anything there. Papa is real good friends with the guy who owns it, Jesse Norman. They play cards together at the VFW every week.

When we got there, we all hopped out of the car, including George Furd, who is also a regular at the Red and White. Kelly and I got ourselves a grape Nehi and banana Moon Pie each. Papa bought us a package of peanuts to put in our sodas and himself a Coca-Cola. Then we lounged around in front of the store, leaning up against the huge plate-glass windows advertising chicken breasts at a dollar forty-nine a pound and Bounty paper towels for ninety-nine cents a roll. While we relaxed, Papa talked to Ernst about his job. Ernst is a policeman.

If there's anything I can say about Papa, it's that he's friends with just about everybody. If he's not a VFW buddy, then Papa goes fishing with him or plays cards with him. But Kelly and I are his best friends in all the world. He's always telling people that.

Ernst told Papa about a new police chief that was pretty strict, and after that I stopped listening and ate my Moon Pie. Kelly, who makes anything good last a long time, just took tiny bites of hers. Then, because my Moon Pie made me thirsty, I drank down my grape Nehi. I set the last of it on the ground so the peanuts would have a chance to start tasting like grape drink and looked in the sand for doodlebugs. Right up next to the building there were a few holes. I played in them with a twig till finally Papa said, "Let's go, girls." And Ernst jumped onto his motorcycle and roared off toward the beach to make sure law and order were being upheld.

Papa got in the car and put in a tape. For Christmas last year Kelly and I got all of Papa's records and copied his country songs off them for him. He said it's the best gift he's ever gotten in all his life. Now he can listen to his music anytime he goes anywhere. "All Around the Water Tank," by one of Papa's favorite singers, was on. We all sang along, including George Furd, who would yelp whenever Papa would yodel. Papa can't carry a note in a bucket, but he can yodel really loud. He's always talking about how he taught his four girls everything they know about singing.

Not to brag or anything, but when Momma and her sisters start singing, they do sound good. Before any of them got married, they would perform live on the radio and were invited down as special guests at the big Baptist church in Daytona all the time. And of course, they sing every year at our family reunions. Momma is always coaching Kelly, Samantha, and our other cousin, Craig, and me in singing. She says with a little work we'll be singing as good as she and her sisters did when they were our age.

Driving with Papa is always fun because unless he is in a real hurry, it takes forever to get where he's going. One time we took off with him to go to the library. It takes Momma or Daddy only three or four minutes to drive there. But not Papa. It was a school night, and Kelly and I had homework to do. On the way over we stopped at the VFW and watched Papa play a few hands of cards, then we stopped at McDonald's and got a bite to eat. After that we headed straight for the library, but got waylaid and had to stop and talk to a couple of friends that Papa saw standing on the street corner. For a while there I thought sure we were gonna go shrimping, but Papa finally called an end to the meeting saying he had to get his favorite girls to the library to get some homework done. We pulled up just in time to see them switching off all the lights. So we headed back for home. On the way to the house we stopped for an ice-cream cone at Wilson's ice-cream parlor and so Papa could chat with Mr. Wilson. Then we had to get gas. After that we checked in at the VFW one more time. That night I did my homework under the covers with a flashlight to see by.

Today wasn't any different. We couldn't go to the beach the downtown way because, sure as we did,

Momma and Daddy would pass us going home. So Papa took all the back roads, and we sang at the top of our lungs all the way.

When we finally arrived at the beach, the sun was pounding down hot. Kelly and I played in the water, and Papa did too. Even George Furd was a sport and swam a little while.

We swam out to the first sandbar, then watched the waves roll in to the shore, standing in the knee-deep water. The sun gave each wave a crown of diamonds. Papa told us about his two friends who were eaten alive when sharks attacked a group of his buddies. It happened years and years ago, and I believe it too. Another one of Papa's friends tells the same story. His name is Elmo and he's missing one arm from the elbow down and a big ol' hunk from one thigh. Sometimes Elmo comes for dinner at our house, and if we're lucky, he'll wear a pair of shorts. He has big white scars on his leg. And as scary as it is to look, you can't help it. Then Elmo will start in singing a song with no tune called "Elmo with the One Elbow." He keeps saying he's going to put it to music, but he hasn't yet. "If I could just play a guitar, I know I could be a star," he says, and then he looks sad and asks for a second helping of dessert.

When we were good and scared, thinking about sharks, we all raced back to the shore.

When the sun was sinking low, we bought sno-cones and climbed into the car. George Furd was tired from a day of resting in the hot sun. Sand was crusted on his black nose. He lay with his head propped out the window and didn't bark at anyone or anything. I would have thought he was asleep for sure if I hadn't heard him growl deep in his throat when he saw a shady-looking character as we were pulling away from the beach.

We passed Ernst sitting on his motorcycle at the side of the road and waved good-bye to him. We were driving on Sandpiper Road. It follows the beach for nearly the entire eastern coast of Florida. There were hardly any cars on the road now because it was so late. As a matter of fact the only car I noticed was a station wagon way on down the road. Papa turned the tape up good and loud, and we sang along with Tammy Wynette.

It was during one of Papa's yodels that it happened. Papa had his head thrown back and he was singing to beat the band. I was trying to harmonize with Kelly. I had my eyes closed from laughing and one hand cupped around my ear trying to hear how I sounded, like I've seen people on TV do. All of a sudden Kelly stopped singing and said, "Papa!" And then we hit the car in front of us.

We weren't going that fast, what with the speed limit being only twenty-five miles per hour on this little two-lane road and the fact that Papa was in the middle of a yodel. It was a hard enough hit, though, that it knocked both George Furd and me onto the floor of the car.

I started laughing.

"Papa," I said. "Ooooh, Papa." And then I noticed that my arm was hurting and so was my head where I had boxed myself in the ear.

Kelly didn't waste any time starting to cry. She kept saying over and over again, "My knee. I think it's broken. My knee."

I looked close at it.

"You're not hurt," I said. "You've just knocked some skin off. Stop bawling and look at my head. Am I bleeding?"

"No," Kelly said. "There's just a handprint on your face. How did you get that?" She wiped at her nose with one arm and investigated the red mark on her knee.

George Furd was whining from the floor of the front seat. One of his teeth was missing.

But the thing that scared me the most was Papa. His face was as pale as a ghost and his hands on the steering wheel were shaking and jerking.

"Papa!" I said. "You're not dead, are you?"

"Papa!" Kelly said, and she was crying again, and sniffing too. She dropped her head onto the back of the seat. "Oh, Papa," she cried. "Please don't be dead."

That's when Ernst pulled up on his motorcycle. He'd witnessed the whole thing.

"Papa?" he said, peering in through the window. "I seen what happened. Are you okay?"

Papa rolled his head to the side and grinned at Ernst.

"Hell, yes," he said.

"How about you girls?" Ernst said. I saw Papa look back at us in the rearview mirror.

"Well," Kelly said. "I do have this scratch on my knee. It's stinging pretty bad."

"Hush," I said, rolling my eyes at Ernst. "You're just fine." I wanted to tell him that my ears were buzzing, but I didn't have a chance.

"I gotta get out of here," Papa said. He was talking loud on account of the tape. It was blaring music out still. "If I get in trouble with the law one more time, they told me they were going to take my license away from me. Sure wish Judge Barron was still working. What's the world coming to when they let a good man like that retire?"

"Just sit tight, Papa," Ernst said. "I gotta check on these other people." He went up to the car ahead of us. The lady who had been driving and her five kids were standing knee high in weeds. She was probably the fattest lady I had ever seen in my life. Just over her shoulder I could see the reeds on the sand dunes. They were swaying in the light breeze. Across the street was a sea of palm fronds. Past that I could see a giant hamburger advertising the best burgers in Florida.

As Ernst got closer to her, the fat lady started whooping, kind of like an Indian from an old Western. The youngest kid was digging in his nose. One of the older boys was singing, "We were in a wreck. We were in a wreck." Everybody there seemed okay.

But I wasn't feeling very good. My neck was starting to ache and my ear still buzzed. And I couldn't believe that Papa really wanted to leave the scene of the crime. Didn't he know that was illegal?

"I gotta get outta here," said Papa.

"We can't leave, Papa," I said. "That's illegal."

"Oooh," said Kelly. "I'm starting to get one of my feelings back."

Papa jumped out of the car. He slammed the door shut, then loped across the road. He didn't even check to see if any cars were coming. He plowed right into the palm fronds and started wading through the waist-deep plants. "Come on, girls," he shouted over his shoulder. "Come on, George. Leah, Kelly, let's go." George Furd leaped out of the car window and trotted after Papa.

"Hey," shouted the lady from the side of the road. She was jumping up and down like she had won a new car or something. "Hey, that old man is leaving. He can't leave. That's illegal. Hey."

"Papa," Ernst called. "Get on back here, Papa. We got paperwork to fill out. You can't leave."

I looked at Kelly, then at the lady standing next to Ernst. She had the nose picker slung up on one hip.

She started over to where Kelly and I sat in the car. She was pointing at me and then to where Papa was cutting through toward the hamburger sign. The fat under her pointing arm swung back and forth. Her shorts were crawling up her white thighs. They looked like a fat blue W on her legs.

"Yuck," I said to Kelly. "How come fat people always wear shorts?"

"She's gonna have us put in jail," Kelly said, not answering me.

"Yuck," I said again. "I don't think I can look at her and that boy at the same time." Suddenly my mouth got all spitty. I felt like I just might throw up all over the blue-green carpet in Papa's car.

"Come on, girls," Papa hollered. Kelly hopped out of the car.

"Papa," shouted Ernst, and I could hear that he was starting to lose his patience. "Papa, get back here right now."

"Wait for me, Papa," shouted Kelly. She wasn't crying anymore. She was running after Papa. She didn't check for cars when she crossed the road either.

"Hey, where are you going?" I said.

The fat lady was standing close to the back car door. I looked at her belly button, straining against the polyester of her red shirt.

"Kelly," I said. "Wait." I closed my eyes and swallowed hard. I climbed over the front seat and got behind the steering wheel. The belly button moved to the driver window. The lady bent down and looked in at me.

"You're not going too?" she said to me. The kid was digging in his nose again. I nodded without looking at her, then I started the car up.

"I'm gonna call the cops on you and that old man," she said, waving her finger in front of my face.

"You don't need to," I said. "We know him." I pointed to Ernst, who was following after Papa, George Furd, and my sister. "Kelly," I shouted around the fat lady. "Kelly, wait." I turned up the tape a little louder.

"I saw the wreck on the highway, but I didn't see anyone pray," screeched the car stereo. I put the car into reverse and backed away from the fat lady. She lumbered beside the car as long as she could, shouting for me to stop. I rolled up the window, then I drove over to the hamburger stand to wait.

June

GEORGE FURD

Well, Papa's driving days were over. Although no one was hurt, including the fat lady and her family, Papa had left the wreck. And even though Ernst had stopped him at the hamburger stand and I had driven back to the scene of the crime with him, things were still looking rather grim. The new chief of police said Papa was a danger to other drivers, a fact proven because he had left an accident. Then the chief topped it all off by saying that Papa was a bad influence to minors, because he had talked Kelly and me into leaving with him.

"You might just as well chop off my legs," Papa said, when Ernst came to pick up his driver's license. "How am I supposed to get around? You know I have an active social life, Ernst."

"Yeah, Papa, I know," said Ernst. "But you're lucky things didn't turn out worse than they did. Be grateful. And listen. We have a good bus system here in New Smyrna."

Papa rolled his eyes. "Buses are for old people," he said.

"Papa, you are a senior citizen. Take advantage of it."

"What?" Papa said. He was getting more and more unhappy. "As soon as I start acting like an old man, I'm gonna curl up in a ball like a roly-poly and die." Papa stomped off toward the house. When he got to our screened-in front porch, he said, "And I will not be caught dead in a bus!"

Ernst laughed and drove away.

And of course Kelly was right with her feelings. Daddy was furious with me. He said an eleven-year-old girl had no business even knowing how to put a car in reverse, and absolutely no reason under the sun to know how to drive a twenty-four-year-old Cadillac. I kept my mouth closed tight about how Papa had been teaching me to drive for nearly three years on our half-acre lot, and that Kelly was getting pretty good at driving too. That old saying, What he doesn't know can't hurt him, seemed almost like Scripture suddenly.

So Papa and George Furd were both pouting. For one whole week they walked to and from the VFW and stayed there from open till close. And when it seemed nothing worse could happen to Papa, another VFW-goer told him to start leaving George Furd at home because his dog's breath was bad enough to kill a horse. Papa said insult upon insult were being heaped upon him. Kelly and I were feeling pretty sad ourselves, what with Papa being gone so much. We were feeling lonesome for him.

Then on Monday afternoon Papa climbed on the

bus to head for the VFW and had to tell George Furd to stay home with Kelly and me. "A man's gotta do what a man's gotta do," said Papa the first time he boarded the very efficient New Smyrna bus system that dropped him off right in front of the VFW. Now he was a pro at riding the bus, and not embarrassed at all.

"Leah and Kelly will take real good care of you," Papa said to George Furd as the bus door closed shut. George Furd's stump of a tail thumped once on the sidewalk. Then the bus roared away, leaving us standing in a cloud of exhaust. We walked the block back home.

Well, I really never thought George Furd would need taking care of. And never once that morning did Kelly get one of her feelings. In fact it was just a normal hot, lazy day.

Momma was off visiting her sister, Aunt Carrie, in Orlando. Orlando is more than two hours away, so when Momma left, she said good-bye for all day long. Daddy was at work. Across the street Brantley and Bryan, the two-year-old identical twins, were running and playing with their mother, Caroline Higley. She was big and pregnant.

A slow breeze was blowing the leaves in the huge oak trees in our yard. There are five of them running the width of our property, planted up near the ditch. Momma's petunias nodded in rhythm with the wind.

Kelly and I were on the front steps, enjoying the warm smells of all Momma's gardenia bushes that edged our driveway and watching George Furd sniff around the mailbox. Out of the corner of my eye I saw Mrs. Rorerson's Aerostar flying down the road. She was going awful fast. Lots faster than she should have been, seeing the speed limit on our road is twenty-five miles per hour because there are so many of us kids living on the block. Suddenly I knew what was going to happen. It was like I had one of Kelly's feelings. I stood up.

"George Furd," I said. "Come on, George Furd." But it was too late. Mrs. Rorerson hit George Furd and sent him flying through the air toward us. He landed in the ditch with a soft plunk. I saw his hind leg slapping at the ground.

I sat back down and watched the rear of Mrs. Rorerson's white van disappear up the road. Her fat arm was slung out the window and she was holding a half-empty bottle of Coke. She didn't even turn around to see what she had hit.

"Oh, no," I said. Tears came to my eyes. Old George Furd was dead. I felt kind of sick. "What are we gonna do? Mrs. Rorerson's murdered George Furd—hit-and-run. Papa is going to die. He is just gonna die."

I stood, pulling Kelly to her feet. She was crying pretty loud, tears running down the sunburned patches on her cheeks, and she kept on saying over and over again, "Poor ol' George Furd. Poor ol' George Furd."

I went over to George Furd and looked at him. His tongue was hanging out of the side of his mouth and there was blood running out of his nose and one ear. Fleas were jumping off him right and left.

"We can't let Papa see him like this," I said. "We just can't." I wiped away a couple of tears that had managed to sneak out. I don't like to cry in front of anybody, especially Kelly, because I'm a year older than she is, and when you're older, you have to keep up an image. Still, the lump in my throat was making it pretty darn hard to swallow.

George Furd was Papa's favorite dog in the whole world. Papa had borrowed five dollars from a Church of God preacher just to buy that ol' dog.

"The onliest time I ever do business with a preacher," Papa had said at the time, exchanging the money for the puppy there on the church lawn. He doesn't really like preachers, not from any church. Come to think of it, Papa doesn't like anything to do with religion, period.

After he picked out the yellow pup, Papa took great pains to name him. He finally decided on George Furd, after an old buddy of his who got hit by a jeep in Korea.

This side of us grandkids, George Furd was Papa's pride and joy. Whenever any of us, Kelly, Samantha, Craig, and I, rode into town with Papa, George Furd got to sit in the front seat. When we were younger, that always made us really mad. Especially since the four of us would be cramped all together in the back. We'd pull at the hair on the back of his neck, making him howl so loud, Papa would have to pull over to see what the matter was.

Well, there'd be no more pulling over to the side of the road now. George Furd was dead. And we were faced with a bigger problem. What should we do with the body?

"Grab ahold of his leg," I said, "and let's pull him away from the road."

"I can't," Kelly said. She was crying so hard, her shoulders were shaking. "I just can't. Oh! He's dead. George Furd is dead."

"You have to," I said. "If Papa were to see George Furd like this, he'd . . . well I don't know what he'd do. You know how he's always complaining about his bad heart. This might be that last straw he's always talking about." Papa is real sure his end is pretty near. He's been prophesying it for years now. Daddy says the old geezer will outlive the world.

"Help me," I said.

We pulled and tugged at George Furd the short distance until we had him out of the ditch and up near the house. He sure was heavy dead.

"What are we gonna do with him?" Kelly said, wiping at her nose with her arm.

I shrugged my shoulders.

"He has to be put someplace Papa won't see him."

"How about we throw him over the fence into the woods?" Kelly said. Our back fence holds the wild growth of trees and bushes from our property. At the very edge are bushes and bushes full of raspberries.

"Naw," I said. "It would attract buzzards."

"He needs a decent burial."

"Yeah. So there won't be a ghost dog floating around." I could see myself going to get in the front seat of Papa's car, if he ever got to drive again, and George Furd's ghost sitting there.

"Hey," Kelly said. "We could put him under the house." Our house stands up on cinder blocks. It's just high enough to crawl under, but you can't sit up straight, once you're there. It is dark and cool, even on hot summer days. When Kelly and I were younger, we'd play house there. Now it is just too tight a squeeze. All that's under the house now are Daddy's tools. It just didn't seem a good place to hide a dead dog.

"No-oh. Papa would wonder what the smell was, and there would be George Furd, stiff-legged, lying under the house, stinking up the yard."

We sat to think for a while.

"Go get a couple of shovels," I said. "We'll bury him in the backyard."

But the grass was too thick. Daddy's always saying there's no thicker grass in the U-nited States when he gets out to mow. Well, Daddy was right about that. We tried four or five places but couldn't get through to the dirt without a lot of grunting and sweating. Papa would be home from playing checkers soon, and something had to be done.

And then it hit me. Out by the shallow well, right next to the garage, there was no grass at all. We could have George Furd buried in a minute.

It took longer for the funeral than it did to dig the hole. Kelly was all choked up and worried that it wouldn't be proper, so when she said the prayer, she asked God to take George Furd up to his bosom in Doggie Heaven, if that was okay with Him. Then she did a lot of crying, and even my eyes got a little wet thinking that there'd be no more George Furd to play with. Finally we put a bouquet of wilted phlox from our yard into the grave with George Furd. We didn't have time to get flowers from Mrs. Comer, and we both knew that whether George Furd was dead or not, it wouldn't be reason enough to pick Momma's gardenias or to pull any roses off the trellis that trains the flowers up one side of the house. Then, handful by handful, we filled in the hole till there was only a mound of white sand near the shallow well. We sat to wait for Papa to come home.

Papa noticed George Furd was missing the minute he walked into the yard.

"Where's that ol' dog of mine?" he said when he got into the house.

Kelly and I looked out the dining-room window to where George Furd was buried.

"Gosh, Papa," I said, crossing my fingers. "I don't know. Probably off visiting some friends."

"Yeah," Kelly said, getting all watery-eyed again. "He's got lots of friends."

At the dinner table Papa asked again. He got the same answer. Papa's chin began to quiver and he said, "Me and that dog's been friends a long time. I sure hope nothing's happened to him."

We thought Papa might forget about George Furd, but he didn't. He called up Aunt Fay and questioned Samantha. When he was sure George Furd hadn't somehow gotten over to her house, he called Craig over at Aunt Nell and Uncle Ray's. Kelly and I hadn't told them anything. You just never know who you can trust to keep a secret. Daddy was starting to get aggravated. He said that no old dog was worth all the complaining he was having to put up with. But that talk didn't stop Papa.

Wednesday night I saw Papa's hand shaking so bad, I thought sure the peas were going to fall off his fork and onto the floor. On Thursday I thought I saw a hint of a tear. Then it got to whenever a dog would bark, Papa would stand in the doorway and call, "George? Is that you, George Furd?"

After a few nights of watching Papa eat dinner

worrying about George Furd being hurt or dead or worse, I started wondering if I was going to get an ulcer.

Almost two weeks after George Furd got killed, Papa, Kelly, and I were out cutting the yard. Once every two months all four of Papa's girls have dinner with him. Papa lets all husbands and kids come, and it's lots of fun visiting with Sam and Craig. We end up singing, and Papa just sits around grinning like he's responsible for us all being so happy. Anyway, tonight we were gathering at our house.

Daddy had given us a deadline for getting the yard work done. We were way behind schedule because we had been taking it easy with Papa, lounging around in the shade, drinking iced tea like it was going out of style. Now it wouldn't be long before Momma and Daddy would be home. It was a hot day and we were hurrying to finish. Papa sent Kelly into the house at least forty times to get water.

"Good Flar-duh water," he said to each glass, holding it up high to the light where it caught the sun's rays and sent off a prism of colors. "There ain't nothing like good Flar-duh water." We just barely beat Momma and Daddy.

I thought what with all the hard work we had done that day, and the fact that Aunt Nell, Uncle Ray, and Craig, Aunt Fay and Samantha, and Aunt Carrie were all over, that Papa would be too tired and too embarrassed to talk about George Furd.

You'd think that he'd let him rest in peace for one night, especially with all the eye-rolling Daddy had been doing. But right in the middle of eating mashed potatoes Papa's eyes got all watery. Right there, with everybody gathered thick around our huge oak table, Papa discovered George Furd's fate.

"I wonder where ol' George Furd is," he said, and then he thought he had it for sure. He slammed his fist on the table. "That ol' dog cost me five dollars," he shouted. "Why didn't I think of it before? Somebody's *stole* that valuable dog."

Aunt Carrie giggled behind her napkin. She always giggles when she's nervous.

Then Papa got real quiet and tears started to run down his face and drip into his snap green beans. "Someone has gone and taken my favorite dog in all my life."

"Puh-lease," Daddy said.

"Andy," Momma said, shushing him.

Papa continued like nothing had been said. He's stubborn that way.

"And me and George Furd was such good friends."

"Daddy," said Aunt Fay. I could see that she was starting to get choked up, and I didn't know if I could handle another crier.

"We had so many good times together. He's out there somewhere tonight, missing me, on account of us being so close all these years. George. George

Furd. Where are you?'' Then he dropped his head into his hands.

Kelly jumped up from the table knocking her slat-backed chair against the wall. I don't know why, but Craig let out a little scream and jumped up too. I guess he's just not used to Kelly's truth-telling.

''Don't say it,'' I said. ''Don't say it.''

''He's dead, Papa,'' she cried. ''George Furd is dead. Mrs. Rorerson ran him down ages ago.''

We all looked at Kelly. She was crying.

''Dead?'' said Aunt Nell.

''Dead?'' said Aunt Fay and Aunt Carrie.

''Dead?'' said Daddy. ''Well, finally.''

I couldn't hardly believe it. Kelly had told. Kelly was running the risk of dropping Papa's last straw. And the silence was awful.

Papa stopped crying and said in a soft, shaky voice, ''Tell me what happened.''

Every aunt and mother looked right at me.

''Hit-and-run,'' I said. ''It was murder.''

''Murder,'' Kelly bawled.

Papa looked from me to Kelly, then back at me.

''We didn't want you to see him that way, Papa,'' I said. ''We knew that you loved George Furd so much.''

''So much,'' Kelly squeaked. She was really crying and talking loud.

''What happened to my poor ol' dog?'' Papa said again, his chin starting to tremble.

"I can't stand it if you start crying again, Papa," I said.

"No, Leah can't stand it if you start crying again, and neither can I," said Kelly. She was crying so hard, she could hardly get her breath. I noticed tears trickling down Aunt Fay's cheeks.

"I won't cry no more," Papa said. "Don't spare me no details. I can take it. Just tell me what happened to my poor ol' dog."

"Mrs. Rorerson mashed the guts out of him with her van," I said.

"Wow," said Samantha. "Squished flat."

"He was bleeding from every hole," Kelly said.

"And his foot was slapping at the ground," I said.

"He was kicking at the air, Papa," Kelly said.

"Are you sure he was dead?" said Craig. He was sitting down again, and both he and Samantha were leaned up on the table looking at Kelly and me. I guess they just couldn't believe how brave we were, even under all this pressure at the dinner table.

"There was blood coming out of his ears and nose," I said.

"Yeah, he was dead," said Craig, shaking his head. "I wonder if we could dig him up and look at him?" Aunt Nell poked Craig with her fork.

"And we didn't want you to see him like that, Papa," Kelly said. "And you were crying at the table every night. . . ."

I started crying then.

"So we buried him," I said.

"Buried him," Kelly said, and then she put her head down in her arms and just cried and cried. Momma patted her on the shoulder.

But Papa didn't cry. He just said, "Tell me where you buried my dog so I can take him out some flowers."

"Out by the shallow well," I said. "He's buried in that soft sand right by the well."

"The well," Kelly said, only it was kind of hard to hear her because her voice was all muffled.

"Out by the shallow well?" Papa said. "Out by the shallow well?"

Samantha stood up to see if she could see out the window, but the backyard was all dark. A moth was beating at the screen trying to get in the house to the light.

"It was the only place we could dig a hole big enough for that dog," I said. "The rest of the place has grass so thick that we—"

"OUT BY THE SHALLOW WELL?" Papa said.

"We'll pick some flowers and put them in a jar and carry them out to ol' George Furd," Kelly said.

"Yeah," I said, sniffing real loud. "We would have done that sooner except we were afraid that you'd figure out what happened." My voice got all squeaky at the end. I wasn't just sad because Papa had found out about old George Furd. I was sad because I knew that I was gonna miss him for a long time.

"We already said a prayer," said Kelly. "All he needs now are flowers."

"And maybe a grave marker," said Craig.

But Papa wasn't interested in taking flowers out to George Furd. He had forgotten all about that. He wasn't interested in a grave marker either. He had forgotten all about Mrs. Rorerson murdering his favorite dog in the whole world.

"I knew it!" he shouted. He stood up and banged his fist on the table. "I knew it!" he said again. "I told everybody there was something wrong with this water. It's dog water. I been drinking dog water!"

Well, after it was all said and done, the worst part about George Furd's dying wasn't that he had been murdered—hit-and-run. It wasn't listening to Papa's crying or wishing his dead dog back. It wasn't even the guilt feelings or wondering if I had an ulcer or not. The worst part was having to carry water from Mrs. Comer's house next door for every meal till the bottled-water company started delivering to us, because Papa wouldn't drink ours anymore.

THE DRIVE

Papa got over George Furd's death as soon as Momma and Daddy switched to city water. He said there was no way he could keep tipping that big ol' water jug every time he needed a drink of water. After enough talking Daddy said he'd buy the whole damn moon if Papa would just shut up. One week later we had city water. Then Grandma got sick, and Momma and Daddy headed off to Jacksonville to get Grandma and to take care of Daddy's brother, Uncle Wing.

See, Grandma was having another dying spell. She has them about twice a year, and Daddy was sure this was the real thing. Daddy's always saying that. It gets Momma all bent out of shape. She says Grandma just has a dying spell so she can see her baby boy and that it's been happening since Daddy moved out to marry Momma. Daddy always brings up that he's been married to Momma what seems an eternity and that this is his only mother and he would never forgive himself if he let her die alone the way his father had. And anyway, his mother is normally a healthy woman. Momma says it's been sixteen years they've been married and that

Grandma was healthy until then. Ever since, she's had a dying spell every few months or so, and I guess that Momma's right because Grandma's been dying for as long as I can remember.

The real trouble with Grandma's getting sick is that every time she does, Daddy's younger brother, Wing, gets to drinking. This time he had hit a couple of guys in the Rusty Anchor Bar and Grill with a barstool, then left without paying his bill. So he ended up in jail. Momma and Daddy were delayed trying to get Uncle Wing home, where Grandma was recovering nicely. Daddy had decided the best thing to be done was to move Uncle Wing and Grandma to New Smyrna, near us, so he could take care of his mother and keep an eye on Uncle Wing. Daddy found a nice little house for Grandma and Uncle Wing just two streets over from us on Pioneer Trail. Momma wasn't real happy about that, but Daddy said what about Papa? Daddy said Papa couldn't get any closer to them unless he moved into their bedroom. Anyway, we expected them home that afternoon.

It was for sure that Kelly and I didn't care that Momma and Daddy were gone. We could do what we wanted and we did. Papa has never been one to keep too close an eye on us. He says it's because he trusts us. And because of his trust we had the run of the house.

We slept till noon every day and went to bed after

two each night. We spent the majority of our time on the beach, with Craig and Sam, and picnicking and visiting with our friends. And now we were bored. Bored because there was nothing left to do. Bored because all our friends on the block—Tom, Otis Mulligan, Shelly Diamond and Rachel Cunningham —were on restriction for going skinny-dipping in the lake behind Shelly's house while her parents were at a party. How Mrs. Comer saw us when it was nearly midnight I'll never know. She must have crept the three houses over in her stocking feet, because we never even knew she was there.

Well, Kelly and I sat in the front yard for who knows how long trying to decide what to do. With only hours left before Momma and Daddy got home from Jacksonville with Grandma and Uncle Wing, we knew it was our very last chance to live it up. Momma was going to kill us sure when she found out about the skinny-dipping incident.

Brantley and Bryan, the two-year-old identical twins, were playing naked in the hose. That's when it hit me. I got up and went in to call Tom, one of my best friends, to ask him to ask his daddy to come over to our house and make a replica key for my daddy's car. Well, Tom said his daddy said he'd make the key if I told him what I wanted it for. So I told Tom to tell his daddy that it wasn't for me. My Momma and Daddy were gone to Jacksonville in Momma's car, and if I didn't start Daddy's car a few times, the battery would run down to nothing, what with it being such an old car and all. And I knew that Daddy didn't want that to happen. So Tom said that his daddy said that was awful thoughtful of me and he'd be over in less than an hour to take care of it. I thanked Tom, but before I hung up, he said, "When you two go out cruising in that car, keep an eye out for Bloomfield. He's back off vacation."

Officer Bloomfield got an award last year for giving out the most tickets. Tom's older brother, Mark, who just got his driver's license, is always having run-ins with Bloomfield.

"It's all set," I said when I came back from inside the house.

"What's all set?" Kelly said. She was stretched out on the lawn, one arm crooked to cover her eyes.

"I've got what we can do. The perfect idea. The grand finale before Momma and Daddy get home this afternoon."

"What's that?" Kelly said. One eye peeked from under her arm.

I leaned close to where she was and whispered, "Me and you can drive Daddy's car downtown. We can drive downtown naked."

Kelly sat right up.

"What?" she said. "Uh-uh. Nope." Then in a relieved voice, "We haven't even got a key. Daddy took the spare one."

I knew why Daddy wouldn't leave a key with

Papa. In fact Daddy even took Papa's keys with him to Jacksonville so Papa wouldn't be tempted. But I wondered why Daddy didn't trust his very own kids.

"I've taken care of that," I said. "We'll have one made. Tom's daddy can do it for us."

"We don't have money to pay Tom's daddy," Kelly said. I could see that Kelly was not going to be easy to convince.

"He'll do it as a favor to Daddy," I said.

"A favor to Daddy?" Kelly said, and rolled her eyes. And then, "No. If we get caught, Momma will kill us twice. We're already in enough trouble. What happens if we get a flat tire? Can you see us out there trying to change it with no clothes on? People would stare."

Kelly has a tendency to imagine every possible thing that could go wrong. She's like Momma that way. Me—I like to use Papa's philosophy: They can kill you, but it's illegal to eat the body.

"We're not going to get a flat tire. Daddy's forever checking all the tires on the car to make sure they're safe."

"Wonder if a tornado sweeps the car into the air and we land in front of the police station. It's been known to happen, you know."

"Only in the movies."

"You don't even have a learner's permit yet." She had me there. It'll be more four years till that day in my life.

"Well, I'm planning on taking driver's education when I get into high school. That's as good as having a license."

"Ha! What about what Momma is always saying about wearing clean underwear. Wonder if we get in a wreck. It's crazy." She got up and stalked into the house.

"You know what Papa always says," I called to her. "They can kill you, but they can't eat the body."

"Oh, yeah, I know," Kelly hollered back.

I followed her into the house. She was sprawled on Momma's new sofa, both feet on the cushions. Momma's real proud of the living room, on account of when Daddy got his bonus this year, she went and bought all new furniture. It's all flowery and pink and blue. Then she and Daddy spent nearly a week repainting the walls a soft blush color and stripping and rewaxing the floors all through the house. Those floors are another thing Momma is real proud of, because they're a golden wood. I don't know why. It's a lot more work. If we had the old carpet down, like over at Tom's house, we'd only have to run a vacuum once in a while.

"Come on, Kelly," I said.

"No."

"See, we won't go naked-naked." I was using my best convincing voice. It works pretty good with Daddy and Kelly, but not at all with Momma. I think she must have used the same one when she was my age.

"We'll wear a coat," I said.

"A coat? It's too hot for a coat," she said, and went into the kitchen and opened the refrigerator.

Well, she was right. It was hot, being in the middle of June and all.

"We'll roll down the windows," I said. "Come on. It's a wonderful idea. Think of telling the story over and over again to all our friends. Think of your 'What I Did for the Summer' essay when we go back to school. It'll be great."

"Wonder if there's a huge tidal wave and every one gets killed except for us and we're left sitting in the car, naked, with only our coats on?"

"If that happens, we'll be glad we spent our last few minutes having a good time. Come on. You worry too much."

"Let me think about it," she said, and stomped up the stairs to our bedroom. Five minutes later she came back into the kitchen. She had a winter coat suspended from each forefinger. My blue wool one and her red wool one. The fake-fur collars moved in the breath of wind that came from the ceiling fan. The large gold buttons shimmered.

"Will these do?" she said.

Tom's daddy was over to our place by 12:31, and by 1:31 the new key was placed in my sweaty palm. He stayed long enough to make sure the key would start the car, then he and Tom left. They were both smiling. Tom was smiling because we had the key and his daddy was smiling because he had done a good deed.

By 1:36 Kelly and I were undressed and in our winter best, backing out of the driveway. Sweat was dripping off our faces and onto the gray fur collars.

"Now, listen," I said. "If we get into any trouble, keep a cool head and let *me* do the talking."

"You can count on me," Kelly said.

We beeped at every house. We yelled at everybody we passed. Kelly barked at all the dogs. We started getting kind of sad that George Furd wasn't with us. He always did the barking before, and we knew that if he were there, he'd be having a good old time too. Maybe even Papa would have enjoyed this. But, no, he had decided earlier that morning to go fishing with Ernst. Those two were probably having lots of fun.

But not this much fun.

We drove out past the library and along Sandpiper Road. The crash of the waves sounded especially cool. The salt air tasted good. We drove past the place where we'd been in the accident with the fat lady and the nose picker. Kelly crossed her fingers for good luck so we wouldn't get into another wreck. We even got to feeling brave and drove past the VFW a few times. Nobody saw us, but that might have been because the VFW is a cinder-block building with very few windows, and we didn't do any horn beeping or yelling. We were gone for what seemed only an hour, when we decided to make a little stop at Wilson's drive-through for an ice-cream cone.

I turned onto Palmetto Road and headed for the parlor. The clock on the bank said it was 98 degrees.

"Whew," I said. "Ninety-eight degrees. And I bet the humidity is a hundred and ten. I would have thought it was hotter than that." Every time I said anything, the fake fur would stick to my lips. I blew. "Pppugh. I sure do wish Daddy would go ahead and get this air conditioner fixed." That's when we noticed Officer Bloomfield. He was sitting a ways up the road in his police car.

"Wave to him and try to look innocent when we drive by," I said. Kelly nodded, and started to wave.

It was too late when I saw the stop sign. There it was, right at the crossroads of Palmetto and India Lane. I don't think the concrete had even had a chance to set yet. They must have put that sign in the ground while Tom's daddy was making us the key. I ran that stop sign right under Bloomfield's nose and screeched to a halt in the middle of the intersection. We both looked back to where the policeman sat. The smell of burned rubber followed us into the car.

"Keep on driving," Kelly said, still waving. "Maybe he didn't notice. Don't stop now." Her face was frozen with an innocent-looking smile. I noticed fake fur on her teeth.

"I can't," I said. "He wants me to pull over."

Kelly started to cry as I edged the car onto the grass at the edge of the road. Wilken's gas station was just ahead of us. A few people there were looking at us.

"Be quiet," I said. "And remember, I'll do the talking."

In the rearview mirror I watched Bloomfield saunter to where we were. The heat was coming up in waves off the blacktop. When I looked out my window, he was bent over staring at me. I could see my face in his glasses. He slapped at the palm of his hand with his ticket book.

"What chew girls doing?" he said, snapping his gum.

"It isn't our fault! It isn't our fault!" Kelly said. "It's Grandma's. She got real sick. So sick, Daddy said it was the real thing. Then Uncle Wing started drinking, and he got put in jail for breaking barstools, and if Momma and Daddy had been home instead of moving them, we wouldn't be here now."

"Be quiet, Kelly," I said, trying to smile, but my

lips kept getting stuck on my teeth. And there was all that fake fur. "Pppugh."

"You ran that stop sign back there, young lady," Bloomfield said.

"They snuck it up on me, sir," I said. "It looks brand-new." I tried to wipe the fur pieces off my face. They stuck to my hand and clung between my fingers.

He nodded.

"Aren't you Andy Orton's kids?" he said.

"Yes, sir, we are, sir," I said.

"It was so hot that we went skinny-dipping," Kelly said. "But we had our underwear on, even though Mrs. Comer says we didn't. And anyway it was so dark, we couldn't see anything even if we had wanted to, and I sure didn't. Now Otis and Tom and Shelly and Rachel are on restriction, and it's not our fault—"

"Shhh!" I said. Officer Bloomfield looked into the car to where Kelly sat crying.

"We're already going to get into trouble for that, even though we had our underwear on. Then Leah" —Kelly jerked her thumb in my direction, and I could see that her hand was shaking bad—"she said, 'You know what Papa always says, they can kill you but they can't eat the body,' and so I said, 'All right, all right, I'll go down there naked.' . . ."

"What's the matter with your little sister there?" Bloomfield said.

I looked at Kelly's face, wet from tears and red from the heat and sunburn, and all sweaty. She looked sick.

"She's gotten some kind of flu," I said. "She's got a real bad fever, and I think it's catching."

He kind of backed away from the car.

"Is that why she's wearing that big coat?"

"Yes, sir."

Kelly was talking real loud now.

"We didn't have anything to do," she said. "But it'll never happen again. I swear I'll wear my clothes from now and forever, underwear and all, if you'll just let us go. Momma and Daddy are on their way home right now, with Grandma and Uncle Wing, and if they find out we asked Tom to ask his daddy to make an extra key so that we could keep the battery built up—"

"Hush, Kelly!" I said. "Pppugh."

"She's delirious," he said.

"It wasn't even my idea. I said we'd get in trouble. I just knew. I had this feeling, and my feelings are always right. We always get caught—"

"I'm just trying to keep her warm," I said. "I was headed for Dr. Cowley's office when I ran that stop sign. I was trying to hurry."

"You catching a fever too?" Bloomfield said, looking at my coat and the sweat running down my face.

"Yes, sir," I said. I put my hand to my forehead. I could feel that my bangs were stuck to my face. I pushed at them with my fingers. Fuzz floated down in front of my eyes and landed on one of the giant gold buttons in my lap. "Yes, sir, I'm feeling a little feverish. Maybe I better just take us home and call Dr. Cowley to come and take a look at us there."

"That's a real good idea," Bloomfield said. "You're looking worse by the minute. I'll lead the way."

He ran back to his car, turned on the lights and siren, and led us right up to our front doorstep, where Momma, Daddy, Grandma, Uncle Wing, Papa, and Mrs. Comer stood waiting for us.

July

WARTS

Daddy said I would be lucky to be driving at twenty-one, and put Kelly and me on restriction for the rest of the month. Both he and Momma were surprised Papa had nothing to do with what Daddy called our latest fiasco. Not to be poking fun at George Furd or showing disrespect to the dead, but you'd think they could just let sleeping dogs lie and forget about my driving at the wreck. But no. Daddy said this driving coupled with the wreck driving was enough to make a sane man crazy. And he wasn't playing around.

We couldn't go out of the yard, talk on the phone, or have any friends over. We almost didn't get to go to Sunday school because we knew people there. Yep, Momma and Daddy were pretty unhappy. All we were allowed to do was go to Grandma's and help her and Uncle Wing move in.

When Grandma and Uncle Wing moved, Grandma brought Cousin Lissie down to help her. She's not really our cousin, but Daddy's. For some reason Wing and Lissie have never gotten along. And the whole week she helped settle Grandma in, those two fought. And fought. And fought. It was awful. Cousin Lissie was sleeping in the spare room at Grandma's, but after two days of constant battling she came to our place to sleep on Momma's new sofa. So with Cousin Lissie right there at our house it was no wonder that it happened. I mean, we were bored nearly to death. And if you were to ask Kelly and me, Cousin Lissie was the worst influence either one of us could have ever had. Just remember this: If anyone tells you frogs won't give you warts, don't believe them.

It had been raining like nothing else, and when Kelly and I didn't think it could get any more boring, we were saved. Our entire yard filled up with tiny baby frogs. I think they rode the raindrops down from heaven, because I cannot figure how they got into our yard.

Well, Cousin Lissie said that Kelly and I could play with all the frogs we wanted, that we had no cause to worry. But Uncle Wing said no, that was wrong. And so was Lissie, and were all the people from Waycross, Georgia, that stupid? Lissie got indignant and got up to leave the room. But before she left, she patted me on the arm and said, "Honey, you certainly won't get warts from playing with frogs. It's a proven scientific fact." Then she tossed her curly hair at Uncle Wing because she had science standing behind her, and left the room.

Well, because we were nearly bored stiff on account of being on restriction, and because Cousin

Lissie had yellow hair with black roots, and Uncle Wing had been drinking because of his mother's recent dying spell, and because Cousin Lissie had gone to night school at Mary Karl Vocational and had walked across the stage to get her diploma that had a red ribbon tied around it, Kelly and I believed her and not Uncle Wing, like we should have. And by the time we got warts, Cousin Lissie had been home for two weeks.

It took a lot of courage to ask Uncle Wing for a cure. After all, we *had* listened to someone else's advice over his. And that person *was* someone he didn't like much. But Uncle Wing was the place to go if you needed a cure. He had only been in New Smyrna one month and had already gotten rid of the fleas off Mrs. Comer's dog by rubbing him with kerosene mixed with a secret ingredient. That's also how he got rid of head lice off Brantley and Bryan, the two-year-old identical twins. He could make the seven-year-itch go away years ahead of time. He prescribed a turpentine string for rheumatism, a copper wire for arthritis, and aloe plants for burns. He could do almost anything. The only problem was getting him to do it now that we had messed everything up by playing with those frogs. It didn't take long to figure out what to do. We'd beg him.

"I don't know, gals," he said, shaking his head sad and sorrowful-like. "Maybe you oughta ask your cousin Lissie."

"Why, she's the one who caused all this trouble in the first place," I said. "I've had enough advice from her to last me forever."

"Seems to me, though, you didn't hear a word I said," he said. "That's what it seems to me." I could tell he was going to make us suffer.

"Aaaw, Uncle Wing, we're sorry. Truly we are," Kelly said. We were at Grandma's house, and Kelly was hanging on the arm of Uncle Wing's easy chair. She put both of her arms around his neck and burrowed her face into the loose skin that hung there. Kelly can cry at the drop of a hat and she means every tear. "It won't never happen again."

Uncle Wing settled back. He pushed his fingers together and tapped his chin with them.

"I want a promise that you won't never take another's advice over mine."

"Oh, we promise, Uncle Wing, we promise," Kelly said.

It's the hardest thing for me to admit that I am wrong. Momma says that me and Papa are cut from the same mold when it comes to pride.

"Now, who said he would take you to the boardwalk right after our family reunion?" Uncle Wing said.

"Why, you did, Uncle Wing," Kelly said.

"And who's been lending a listening ear this past little bit whilst you been in the doghouse?"

"You have," Kelly said. Her chin was starting to quiver.

"And now look how you've hurt me." Uncle Wing dabbed at his eyes. "What with me trying to be your friend and all."

"We're sorry we're sorry we're sorry we're sorry."

I never said a word.

Uncle Wing wrote the cure down for us, and we memorized it, then flushed it down the toilet. The flushing was part two of the cure. Part one was memorizing what the cure was. Part three was waiting for a full moon. Part four was drinking lots of liquids. It was going to be a cinch.

We were lucky. A train wrecked in Oak Hill a few days later on a full-moon night, and Daddy had to go. When you work for the railroad, there's no telling what you might have to do or when they might call you.

Momma and Daddy argued about the car. Earlier that morning Momma had been giving Mrs. Comer driving lessons. Mrs. Comer is always asking Momma to carry her up to the Rexall drugstore, ten minutes before it closes, for snuff, or having her run out to the grocery store for a can of something or other right when we sit down to dinner.

Momma said it was her Christian and neighborly duty to teach Mrs. Comer to drive, even though she knows that little old lady can't even see an inch in front of her face in the broad light of day. Kelly and I tried to warn her, but Momma didn't hear. She never listens to a thing we say.

Well, when they pulled into the yard, Momma said, "Hit the brakes." I heard her from where I was sitting on the screened-in porch. I guess Mrs. Comer got overly excited, because she slammed on the gas. She ran over one of Momma's prize gardenia bushes, smashing it flat, and finally stopped in the backyard when she hit the clothesline pole, knocking it whopper-jawed and tearing out one of the headlights on the car. If George Furd hadn't already been in Doggie Heaven, Mrs. Comer would have sent him there sure. Momma started wishing she had maybe kept her ear open a crack when we were talking. Kelly and I tried not to have that I-told-you-so look, but it was pretty darn hard, seeing that we had nearly told the future.

Daddy said later he didn't care if there *was* only one headlight, he was taking the car. He said he might work for the railroad, but there was no way he was riding twenty-five miles up to Oak Hill on a train when he could drive, and Kelly and I spent all day drinking all the water, and lemonade, and Cokes we could hold. Pretty soon Momma said that we were going to rot all our teeth out, and did we like the idea of smiling big, black, holey smiles on picture day at school? Kelly said no, and before she could say any more, I elbowed her in the gut. But

Momma was too worried about her gardenia bush to listen for an answer.

Kelly and I made sure Momma and Papa were asleep before we left the house. Scarier than being caught by Momma was the thought that Mrs. Comer might see us. She might not be able to see good enough to drive, but she had already proven that she could see in the dark when she caught us skinny-dipping. Kelly and I kept our eyes peeled, watching her place to see if maybe she was watching us. It was midnight, and her old rooster was crowing. He's as mixed up as she is. It was cool outside. The ground was wet with dew and there were frogs croaking, and before long our warts would be gone and I couldn't hardly wait.

We went over Uncle Wing's cure one more time to make sure we had it right. He had given it to us two days earlier and we had rehearsed it over and over. We couldn't afford to mess this up. We had a whole month before the next full moon.

"Let's check 'em off," I said.

"Okay," Kelly said.

"Got a dishrag?"

"Yeah."

"You tied a knot for each wart?"

"Yeah."

"Me, too," I said.

The moon was white gold reflecting off the pavement of the street, and there were so many lightning bugs flitting around, it looked like some of the stars had dropped down closer to watch us. I had never realized you could see so clearly on a full-moon night. The oak trees in the front yard glimmered and waved and cast shadows like dark ghosts running across the yard. Momma's gardenia bushes, the ones that were left standing, were dark, except for the white flowers that seemed to bob-float in the air.

It took a long time to decide who would go into the road first. Finally we took ahold of each other's hand and went together.

"Well," I said. "This is it."

"Yeah," Kelly said. "This is it."

"Pretty soon we won't have a single wart left."

"That's right. Not one left."

"You gotta go?"

"You're not just kidding," Kelly said. "You?"

"I think I'm gonna bust a gut," I said. And I meant it.

We stood silent in the middle of the road looking at each other. The moon dripped around us, setting everything aglow with its light. I could see the flowers on Kelly's nightshirt. Even the mailbox was shining, and ORTON, ROUTE 1 BOX 83 was as easy to read as if it had been day.

"Well, this is it," I said.

"Yeah, this is it."

"Wait a minute. Did you dig a hole to bury the dishrags?"

"I thought we could use the one Mrs. Comer dug up when she spun out in the front yard."

"Good idea," I said. And then after a second, "This better work."

" 'Course it'll work," Kelly said. "Has Uncle Wing ever lied to us before?"

"Well," I said, "he hasn't had much of a chance to. He's only been here a little while. It's just that this doesn't seem like it'll make our warts go away."

"Aaaw, you're just like Momma, Leah. You don't believe nobody."

"And you're just like Daddy, Kelly. You believe anything anyone says."

"This isn't anyone," Kelly said. "This is our uncle Wing."

"I just got the feeling that Uncle Wing is pulling our leg. You know his feelings were hurt pretty bad. Maybe he got to thinking and decided to pull a joke on us."

"He wouldn't do that."

"Yeah," I said. "I guess you're right. So this really is it."

"Yeah," Kelly said. "This really is it."

I hiked up my nightshirt. Kelly did too. We squatted in the middle of the road on a full moon at midnight, each clutching a knotted dishcloth. It was a real relief till Kelly said, "Hey, I think I hear a car."

I listened. I could hear it too.

"Hurry, Kelly, hurry. If anybody sees us . . ." I

was so scared, I almost started crying. Kelly was bawling already. Neither one of us could do anything but squat. Cousin Lissie, it was all her fault. If she hadn't been so high and mighty with her education and yellow hair with black roots, this would have never happened. There she was, safe and sound in Waycross, and here we were, peeing in the middle of the road.

"Run!" I said. "Run!"

But it was too late. The car rounded the curve, and I saw it only had one headlight and I knew it was Daddy.

FAMILY REUNION

One week after the Fourth of July celebration we have our two-day family reunion. Relatives from all over Florida, Georgia, and Alabama gather to visit, talk about what has happened the past year, and occasionally gossip about each other when the person they are talking about is nowhere near. There's always tables and tables of food. A bunch of people bring their six- and twelve-string guitars, and we all sit out under the oak trees and sing loud and long. When the mosquitoes finally start biting, about an hour after the sun sets, we call it a day till the next afternoon. That way everyone has a chance to get together in groups and plan for the next afternoon's entertainment. Usually there will be singing or dancing, and sometimes if we're really lucky, both.

Once when I was about seven, Papa gathered up all us grandkids and taught us a song to perform for the family. He copied the idea and tune from a cereal commercial. Papa strummed lightly on the guitar while we all sang,

"Spell the Post Alpha-Bits, c-a-r-t cart.
Sugary Alpha-Bits, f-a-r-t fart . . ."

We didn't even get to sing the whole thing because of people either laughing or telling Papa it was a sin to teach a bunch of kids to talk that way. Every reunion people remember that song, especially Momma, and we're always asked to sing it again. But that was a once-in-a-lifetime performance.

A real regular on the entertainment agenda is Momma and her sisters. They've been singing together since before Aunt Fay could walk really good, and, like good wine, Papa says, they get better and better each year. Aunt Nell will play the guitar and they'll sing songs they wrote themselves, usually about divorce, because the writers in the group know all about living alone since they both got divorced not too long ago. Momma says Aunt Fay got divorced because Uncle Leon was nearing forty, which makes no sense to me, and Aunt Carrie got divorced because she couldn't be outdone by their younger sister, who is always doing things up really nice, at least according to Momma. Aunt Carrie, though, has no children and Aunt Fay does have Samantha.

This year the reunion was to be in New Smyrna at Aunt Fay's big house. She did pretty good after her divorce, because she ended up with the house, the car, and my cousin Sam, from Uncle Leon. She doesn't even have to work, she just does because she got tired of sitting around with nothing to do but eat, she said.

Aunt Fay and Sam live nearly smack dab on the ocean. They're just three blocks away. Their house is huge, because before the divorce Uncle Leon was a very successful insurance salesman and he made lots of money. Momma says Uncle Leon bought Aunt Fay everything she could ever want, and looking at her house you'd believe that. A porch runs around three sides. There's all this wicker furniture everywhere. The windows dip almost to the porch floor itself. And the inside. The inside of Aunt Fay's house is full of beautiful antiques. I know it sounds kind of funny to hear a kid say that the furniture is nice, but it is. It's all this golden-color wood, which matches the floors and reminds me of honey. And every few years or so Aunt Fay has decorators come in and change all the fabrics and stuff like that. Whenever one of the decorators comes over, they always oooh and aaah. Right now, all of Aunt Fay's colors are blues and mauves and dusty greens.

Sometimes when Kelly and I come home from spending the night with Sam, Momma will give us the "Money Lecture." She says lots of money and lots of nice things aren't necessarily that wonderful. She says would I change my daddy for all that Samantha has? And I have to say no.

See, Uncle Leon just up and said he wanted to be free, to walk clear of Aunt Fay, with the wind blowing in what was left of his hair. He told Aunt Fay that it was her and all her demands that had him nearly bald from worry. I know because when all this divorce stuff was happening, Aunt Fay would come with Sam to our house and talk to Momma. Kelly, Sam, and I would sit mouse-quiet at the top of the stairs and listen to what was going on.

So, when the divorce was final, Uncle Leon did walk. Straight to the bus station, where he met a young redheaded girl, and they left for Saint Augustine together. I seen them with my own eyes. Uncle Leon and the girl, who kept smiling up at him, sitting there on the bench waiting for the bus. Aunt Fay was supposed to give me a dollar for seeing what was happening with Leon, but when Kelly and I told all, she started crying and drinking and forgot all about paying us anything. That night she wrote her first song about divorce. It's a real favorite at the reunions, because it makes everybody cry.

For a week before anybody showed up, Momma, Aunt Nell, and Aunt Fay worked getting things ready. Aunt Carrie wasn't to arrive till reunion day 'cause she lives in Orlando and she just couldn't take off work. Anyway, every day they cleaned and cleaned Aunt Fay's two-story house. Aunt Fay usually has a maid come in three days a week, but she said no maid could be trusted to get the house in the kind of order she wanted it in. So they scrubbed the wood floors till you could see your face in them. They washed all the sheets on all the beds, in all five bedrooms, even the ones that hadn't been slept in for more than a year, and sprayed lilac perfume on them because Aunt Nell said that she had read that movie stars in Hollywood do that. They even cleaned places people wouldn't see, like behind the toilet, right next to the wall. And under the fridge, and behind the stove. It was just too much cleaning for me. Kelly and I helped Samantha, because we knew Aunt Fay would come wipe her hand over the canopy bed and tall oak chest, checking for dust. She did surprise us, though, when she dug under Sam's bed with a yardstick and pulled out a whole bunch of clothes Sam had been wondering about. Finally, much to our relief, Momma and Aunt Fay opened all the windows wide, and the smell of the ocean drifted in, making everything seem warm and sunny.

Then they were off to our place, where they baked pies and fried chicken and made dressing, so as not to mess up what they had done at Aunt Fay's house. But mostly that week they sang together. They practiced the old songs they sang at every gathering, and they practiced new songs that they had written just that year.

For one week Kelly, Samantha, and I squished three in my bed because both Craig and Sam slept over. Craig got to sleep in Kelly's bed alone because he's the only boy, but none of us minded at all.

Each night, after we'd go to bed, Aunt Nell would play the guitar and they'd start singing, their voices blending like melted chocolate. They would laugh and carry on together. Sometimes Papa would yodel along with them, and I could hear Daddy talking about how wonderful "his Laura" was. In my mind I could see him touching her shoulder, the way he touches something he's proud of, and running his hand down her arm. For that whole week our house was full of so many good smells and feelings and laughter that it nearly glowed. And in all my life, going to sleep to my family's singing made going to sleep the best part of the day.

On the Friday after the Fourth our family started arriving at Aunt Fay's house. Cousin Lissie from Waycross was the first to get here. This time her hair was red and she brought a guy who she introduced as "Myron the man in my life." Kelly and I stayed away from her and stuck close to Uncle Wing till he and Cousin Lissie started fighting. Myron just sat around googly-eyed, staring at Lissie. I guess he didn't know that her hair was once blond and that she didn't know a thing about frogs, or else he'd have stayed in Georgia. Every once in a while he'd grin at Kelly and me and show his big teeth. They were yellow and stuck out some. The worst part was that every time he would laugh or smile, spit would string from one lip to the other, almost like a spiderweb. It kept bubbling up and collecting in the corners of his mouth. I rubbed my own hand over my lips, hoping he'd get the hint, but he never did.

By three o'clock nearly everyone was there. Kelly, Samantha, Craig, and I climbed up into Sam's tree house. She is pretty lucky, with this tree house and all. I guess if I could have anything that she has, I'd take a tree house like hers. But my daddy is not a handyman.

Uncle Leon built the tree house for Sam on her ninth birthday, and right after that he left. Aunt Fay said while he was drawing up plans for the old tree house, he was drawing up plans on leaving town.

Anyway, Sam's brought in all her books, and there's even an old mattress to lie on so you can read in comfort. She has a whole bunch of comic books, her very own chalkboard with chalk, and an old flashlight that works pretty good except you have to shake it a lot. There used to be a tire swing that hung from one of the branches that faces the front road, but one time we were pushing Kelly in it really hard and the rope broke. Kelly bounced down the driveway quite a ways, then toppled over on her back. Every time I thought about it the next day at school, I laughed, till finally one of my teachers asked what was so funny. The broken rope still hangs from the limb.

At the base of the tree are two plaster pink flamingos. They used to be Aunt Fay's favorite things in the yard. She named them Fred and Marsha. They stand with one leg tucked up under them, just like real flamingos do, only it looks like Fred is smiling and like Marsha is guarding the backyard. I don't know why she keeps them, because she's always saying how they remind her of Leon her Ex. Momma said that Uncle Leon bought them for Aunt Fay as a wedding present because before they got married, Aunt Fay said that all she ever wanted her whole life was two pink flamingos to stand in her very own backyard. I guess Uncle Leon really loved Aunt Fay when they first got married, because Momma says those birds stood in the living room of every apartment they lived in till they finally got a place of their own.

Now, sitting up in the tree house, we could see everything that was going on really good, and whenever a kid that we liked drove up with some of the family, we'd call out for them to come on up.

I watched Momma and her sisters running around laughing and joking and putting food out on the tables. There was so much, it didn't seem possible we could eat it all, but I knew that by tomorrow, when everyone was driving off, there'd be nothing in the pans for them to carry home. From where I was standing, looking down on the whole thing, I could even see the flies buzzing around. The iced tea cast golden shadows onto the mashed potatoes. There were heaps of barbecued beef ribs with sweet sauce dripping into puddles on the plates. The hams had pineapple rings baked on them, and there were hills of corn on the cob and mounds of potato salad.

There was chicken fried the way only Momma knows how, and sweet potatoes with marshmallows baked crunchy and brown. There were even a couple of platters of fried bass that Kelly, Papa, and I caught just for this occasion. And for dessert there were so many pies and cakes that it took one table to hold it all. All this was crowded on one porch, on long brown tables borrowed from the Baptist church.

Kids who were too small to climb up to where we were, or that we didn't like and didn't want to be where we were, stood along in lines waiting for the blessing to be said so they could eat. Every once in a while one of the men would grab a small bite of something, only to be whacked at by one of the women.

When the blessing was to be said, we all climbed down from where we were perched and gathered close to the front porch to where Great-grandma Nettie sat. She's really skinny and wears old-fashioned dresses and a sweater, no matter how hot it is outside. Since she's the oldest left in Momma's family, she presides at all our reunions. She is Grammy's mother, and now she lives in Pensicola with one of her boys. Grammy didn't have any sisters, and she was the youngest of eight children, but she was still the first to die. Papa steers clear of Great-grandma Nettie because he says she blames him that Grammy died, but he still has a lot of respect for her. I guess that's because he loved her daughter so much.

We all gazed at Great-grandma Nettie. She looked back hard, with eyes as blue as the fishing pond we visit with Papa. Finally she lifted her hand and called out for Uncle Dan to say grace. Then it was time to eat.

And that's when the trouble began. I should have known there was going to be trouble when I got a sick feeling in the pit of my stomach. I was back in my place in the tree house, right next to the window. There must have been ten of us in there, so it was kind of crowded and hot. I was eating my dessert first. Pecan pie. It's my favorite, and with all those people there I knew I had to eat my fill now or do without. Anyway. I was sitting there, thinking how I might get seconds when I glanced up just in time to see Uncle Leon, the redheaded girl, and a little boy come walking up the sidewalk. The yard at Aunt Fay's house is nowhere near the size of ours, but this sidewalk does go down the entire edge of the property, right past all the tables that were set up on the porch and into the backyard, where it ends at the back door.

It had been three years since I last saw Uncle Leon at the bus station. None of us thought we'd ever see him again, and here he was coming to our very own family reunion, and bringing the red-headed girl and a little boy that looked a lot like Uncle Leon, except his face was splashed with freckles and his hair was the color of copper.

"Oooooooo," I said. "Aunt Fay is not going to like this. No not one bit."

"What's that?" Kelly said. She was eating a deep-dish Georgia peach pie.

I nodded with my head to the little group, now parading down the driveway.

"Why, that's my daddy," said Samantha. But she didn't do anything except stand at the window, like the rest of us, and stare.

"What in the world is he doing here?" said Craig. "And who are those two with him?"

Uncle Leon was holding on to both the red-headed girl and the little boy. She was dressed to the hilt, including a hat with a green ribbon and a dress made from the same shiny-green material. The little boy had on a suit with a tiny bow tie. I was thinking of how long of a walk it must have seemed to them, passing all those people, and I wondered if Uncle Leon felt that way.

"She looks beautiful," said Sam.

"She looks overdressed," I said. "I wonder why Uncle Leon didn't tell her you just wear everyday clothes to these get-togethers, and not something for church at Christmastime?"

By now they were underneath us and I knew they

were being noticed because everything was getting quiet. The last thing I heard was Aunt Fay saying, "Who? Look at who?" and then, "Oh, my landsake."

We all crept to the other window and looked down. They were standing right next to a big petunia flower bed. I had a perfect view of the tops of their heads, Leon's bald spot, the hat of the girl, and the copper color of the boy. Fred and Marsha stood beside them, smiling and guarding.

"I've come so you can meet my new family," said Uncle Leon. "This is my wife, Margaret May, and my little boy, Charles Leon the second. Say how do you do, Charlie."

Charlie tipped an imaginary hat and said, "Whodee-do." And then it was quiet again except for when Papa and Uncle Wing thundered out the back of the house. I heard the screen door slam and then Papa said, "What in tarnation is it so quiet for? I thought we were reunion-ing."

"They missed us, Papa," said Uncle Wing.

I couldn't see what was happening, but I could imagine. Uncle Leon looked over to where Papa and Wing stood.

"Hey, Papa," he said. "I come to show you my new family."

Papa came leaping down the stairs two at a time and grabbed Leon by the arm and pumped his hand up and down and up.

"So you have, so you have," Papa said, and then everyone came back to life again. Someone offered Margaret May a place to sit under an awning Aunt Fay had put in so people could sit cool and comfortable, and Charlie followed his momma while Uncle Leon dished up three plates of food. He was talking to nearly everyone like he had never been gone at all. Talking like he wasn't standing in the yard with two people who maybe shouldn't have been there.

I leaned in the tree house and looked at Samantha.

"Your daddy's here," I said.

"So?" said Sam.

"So aren't you gonna go down and see him?" said Kelly.

"I seen him already."

"You've not seen him for three years," I said.

"I seen him out the window," said Sam, "and that's good enough for me right now."

We all looked back out the window, giving Sam the best place to stand.

"Hey," said Papa. "Let's get some entertainment going here. I feel like hearing some music whilst I un-lax." He looked over to where Momma was standing talking low to Aunt Fay. Aunt Nell and Aunt Carrie were standing close by.

"Girls," said Papa. "Sing for us."

Even from where I was, I could see that Aunt Fay didn't want to do any singing. In fact she had the same look on her face that she had the day Kelly and I told her about Uncle Leon at the bus station. Suddenly, though, she straightened up, and after a minute Aunt Nell got the guitar. They went and stood on the stairs that led into the backyard. A trellis of ivy grew up onto the porch roof and curled down and around the rain gutter. Everyone got real quiet. Some people stood eating, ready to listen, not quite ready to quit with the food. Others gathered in little groups and sat on lawn chairs and in the grass.

> *"On a cold and windy night he left me,*
> *Left me sitting all alone.*
> *The baby was crying, I thought I was dying,*
> *I was sitting all alone.*
> *Took me a while to get my life back together,*
> *I was sitting on my own.*
> *But I'm gonna make it, yes I'll be able to*
> *make it.*
> *I'll not be sitting on my own*
> *All alone,*
> *All alone.*

(Chorus)

> *"Oh, men, what good are they? Yes*
> *men, sweet talk is all they do.*
> *Men, say that they love ya,*
> *then men, well then they leave ya,*

Men, I guess that I am through.
With men.
Aaah, with men.

"My baby he's done gone and left me,
Sitting on my own.
He said that he would always love me.
He lied, now I'm sitting on my own.
The house seems so quiet
Now I'm sitting on my own
Maybe someone will buy it so
I'll not be sitting on my own.
All alone,
All alone.

(Chorus)

"He left with a girl from the station here in town
Yes, he left me standing in the door
Wearing my wedding gown
He went up the coast,
Celebrate with a toast
I am free, I am free
Yes I am.
And I'm gonna make it,
Yes, I swear I will make it
I'll succeed, I sold that old wedding gown.

On my own,
On my own."

(Chorus)

Margaret May's face turned red, redder than even her hair. I didn't blame her at all for being embarrassed. I would have been too. I started wishing, even though it had happened years before, that I hadn't told Aunt Fay the things I'd seen with Kelly at the bus station.

Momma looked uncomfortable. In fact everyone was fidgeting and talking low. As soon as the song was over, Momma and her sisters started right into another song, blending in lots of others that they had written.

The day went on without much more happening, except at the very end. That's when Uncle Leon put two and two together and realized Samantha was up hiding in the tree house. He asked and asked Aunt Fay where Sam was, but Aunt Fay never had anything to say to him. All day long we climbed up and down, up and down, hauling things in for Sam to eat and drink and for us to play with. She didn't want to come out and risk getting caught by Uncle Leon. I didn't quite understand why she felt that way, but we just kept her informed as to what was happening, and she kept out of sight.

It wasn't until Uncle Leon was getting ready to leave that he figured out where Samantha was.

"Come on down, girl," he called up the tree. He was standing next to Fred and Marsha, and holding on to Fred's head.

Sam ignored him.

"I know you're up there. You can't stay up there all night long. The mosquitoes will eat you alive."

"Yes, I can," Sam said to me.

That's when Aunt Fay showed up and started fussing and fighting with Uncle Leon. I guess she had been saving up speaking to him until right then. They were shouting a lot of not-so-nice things when Sam finally leaned her head out the window.

"Why don't you both just shut up," she said. "I'm sick of hearing you. And I will not be coming down." And I could tell by the firmness of her voice that she meant business.

Uncle Leon and Aunt Fay were so shocked that neither one of them spoke for quite a while. When they finally did, it was under their breath so none of us could hear what was going on.

"Listen hard," Sam said, and so Kelly, who can hear a pin drop for a mile, leaned out the window and listened. But all she heard was "She's my daughter too" and "You should have thought about that before you left."

By this time most everyone had gone into the house or to other relatives' homes to get ready for bed. A cool breeze was blowing in off the ocean, so the mosquitoes weren't hardly bad at all. And also we had a Pic burning on both windows. We always save them from when we go to the drive-in so we can use them later if we decide to sleep outdoors. Those things work really good, and I know why. If a person can't breathe that Pic air, neither can a mosquito.

We heard the screen door slam shut, and I looked out the window. Uncle Leon, Fred, and Marsha were standing under the tree. Aunt Fay was gone. Margaret May sat on the porch, with Charlie asleep on her lap. She looked real sad.

"Tell Samantha to come on down," Uncle Leon said.

I stuck my head in the tree house.

"Your momma's gone in and your daddy wants to talk to you," I said.

Sam walked slowly to the window.

"I'm not coming down," she said.

"Just talk to me," said Uncle Leon.

"Why should I?"

"Because I'm your father."

"So?"

"So. So show me some respect and let me talk to you face-to-face."

"I don't owe you any respect," said Sam. "You left."

Uncle Leon just looked up at her. All of us—Sam,

Craig, Kelly, and I—were squeezed out the one window, staring down. All the other kids had gone on to other places to sleep.

The sun was setting and the sky was splashed pink and gold. I could hear the waves crashing on the shore not too far away. Fred and Marsha were shining in the light, almost glowing.

"I did what I thought was right," Uncle Leon said.

"You did what you wanted," said Sam, "and you didn't ever think of me. Only yourself." I thought I heard Margaret May crying and then I realized it was Sam.

"I thought of you every day."

"You didn't think of me once. And you don't love me. You only love her and him. Not me. Not me ever."

"That's not true. I do love you. I just had to go. I wasn't happy. Your momma is a hard woman to live with." And then Uncle Leon started climbing up to where we all were.

"Don't you never say nothing bad about my momma. She's always been here for me. Not you. Not you never. You're no father. You're not my father. Stay away from me."

"I'm coming up there, and I'm going to talk to you."

"Help," screamed Samantha. "Momma, help."

And then like spilling water spreads, we all got scared and before I knew it, we were all screaming.

Uncle Leon stopped climbing the stairs. He was close enough, I could almost touch the shiny part of his head. He looked at me, only for a second. His face was dark and angry. Embarrassed. Then he looked at Samantha.

"You're right," he said. "You're not my daughter. You are your mother's."

Then he backed down until he was standing in front of Marsha. He swung with a fury I'd never seen him have before and knocked Marsha down. He stepped twice on her plaster belly and stomped to the porch where Margaret May sat open-mouthed.

"Let's go," he said, taking Charlie from her. "Let's go home."

Margaret May sobbed into her hands.

"Do go," screamed Aunt Fay. She was on the porch, my family gathered around her. "Go and never come back."

Uncle Leon and his family walked down the sidewalk.

When she couldn't see her daddy anymore, Samantha sat down on the mattress and cried.

The next day, after all the family had left, Aunt Fay went out and planted Marsha back beside Fred.

"I hope that man never comes back," said Aunt

Fay. "This is just to remind me, every time I think of that man, that I do not want him back."

"Especially now that he has that wife and kid," said Papa.

Aunt Fay ignored him.

Not long after our family reunion Samantha got a letter from her daddy. She wouldn't tell Kelly and me what it said, and we never felt it right to ask. It was something we just couldn't understand, with our momma and daddy together and best friends.

Shortly after the letter arrived, Sam rode her bike over to our house. She had a big bag tied to the back fender.

"I'm going to the dump," she said. "You wanna come with me?"

"Yeah," I said, and we got our bikes out of the garage.

"Whatcha got in that bag?" Kelly said.

But Sam didn't answer.

The sun beat hot on my head. The dump is only a couple of miles from where we live, so it didn't take too long to get there. We passed Wilson's ice-cream parlor and I mentioned that I wouldn't mind treating everyone to something cool and sweet on the way home. I was trying to get Samantha to talk, but it didn't work. We rode past the stop sign I had run earlier that summer. Officer Bloomfield wasn't there today. I felt pretty happy about that. We turned down Adison Avenue and raced past cow and horse pastures and a huge cabbage field. The delicious smell of dirt and growing things filled the air. We passed Lake West and splashed through a creek. On the left-hand side of the road was the cemetery where all my family has been buried for generations. Not too much farther and then we were there. The New Smyrna City Dump sign swung on a cable. We parked our bicycles here and climbed over the wire.

Everything was peaceful and quiet, except for the seagulls that dipped to the ground every once in a while in their search for food.

Sam surveyed the area and finally pointed to a tall pile of trash.

"Let's go over there," she said.

We walked to where she had pointed, scanning the ground for anything that might be worth taking home. The dump is a good place to find treasures, depending on what your needs are for that day, but I couldn't find anything.

At the top of the pile Sam opened her bag and took out Marsha.

"I'm tired of listening to Momma talk about how this old thing reminds her of my daddy," she said.

She stuck the iron-rod leg into the ground and stood back for a minute. Then she turned around and we all started for home, leaving Marsha to guard the dump.

August

THE WEREWOLF

I told them not to make us baby-sit, but whoever listens to kids?

"If anything happens," I said, "if we're killed or mangled or sucked dry by a vampire . . ."

Momma rolled her eyes at the ceiling.

". . . or our throats are ripped out by a werewolf, just remember—I told you so."

"Take your feet off that sofa," Momma said, and she clicked into the kitchen to see if the oven was off. She was wearing these new high-heeled shoes with pointy toes. They had little red bows on them. "You pay a price for beauty," Momma had told Aunt Nell earlier that day when she had showed her the shoes, "and these shoes nearly kill me."

"Papa will be here before seven to check on you three," Momma said from the other room, "and Nell wants Craig in bed no later than nine o'clock. Nine-*oh*-clock." She came back into the living room, dabbing at her lipstick with a paper towel. "I told you to take your feet off my new sofa," she said, swatting at me.

"In that movie, *I Was a Teenage Werewolf,*" Kelly said, "Michael Landon ripped that girl to pieces."

Kelly is a scaredy-cat and she believes movies are true. If it wasn't for me being so brave and all, she would go around crying and shaking all the time.

"I'm not scared at all about vampires," I said, scratching my mosquito bites, "because you can ward them off with garlic. But werewolves . . . they rip your guts out." I'd seen it happen right on HBO in *An American Werewolf in London.*

"I know you're trying to get Kelly scared so I have to stay home tonight, but it's not going to work," Momma said. "The two of you are old enough to watch Craig, and like I told you before, your grandfather will be coming home."

"Every time that kid comes over here, we get into trouble," Kelly said.

"You two get into trouble whether Craig's here or not," Momma said. I knew she was thinking about us trying to get rid of our warts, which by the way were gone. Momma had told Daddy to spank us good and hard, but Daddy said being caught in the act was punishment enough. He still laughed whenever he thought about it. Kelly and I didn't think it was that funny. Especially when Daddy would tell his friends and say, "Yessiree, buddy. I saw *three* full moons that night."

"Kelly's right, Momma," I said. "Remember the last time you made us watch him? He did a *Miami Vice* dive out the front door and tore the screen half off the porch trying to save us from robbers and killers."

"And," Momma said, "if I remember correctly, Leah, you two told him there was an escaped convict hiding in the sun room. Now"—Momma pointed hard at us to emphasize each word—"you two are going to watch your cousin until Papa gets here from the VFW, and you might as well make your minds up to it."

"If we're dead when you get home," I said, "if there are dead bodies strung from A to Israel, then you'll be sorry."

"If you don't get your feet off my new sofa, then *you're* going to be sorry." And since it sounded like she meant it that time, I got up and went over to the TV; I plopped down and turned on the set. Kelly was lying on the floor looking through the movie guide. Tonight was Fright Night on HBO.

"Forty-five more minutes," she said, looking at her watch, "and the fun begins. They're playing some of the oldies and then ending up with some of the Freddie and Halloween movies. First thing on is Lon Chaney, Jr., in *The Return of the Werewolf.*" She squinted one eye and pulled her hands up into claws. "YEEEOOOOW!"

Momma moved into the dining room and back into the living room, then checked out the window. She and Aunt Nell were meeting Daddy and Uncle

Ray at a special railroad workers' assembly, where they were going to be served dinner and everything.

These meetings happen about once every three months, and every time, Craig has to come and stay with us. Kelly and I figure that Uncle Ray's momma is just too smart, or else she'd be baby-sitting him.

"You three don't sit up all night watching those darn horror movies and scaring yourselves to death," Momma said. "And take care of Craig. Don't let him get into trouble this time. I am holding you two responsible."

Just then Aunt Nell pulled into the driveway. I could hear Craig hollering out the window. He was firing his plastic gun at escaped convicts.

"Great," I said, rolling my eyes at Kelly.

"POW! POW! WATCH OUT, LADY. THEY'RE HEADED TO YOUR SIDE OF THE CAR! DRIVE FAST AND WON'T NOBODY GET HURT!" He was sitting in the backseat, and I know why. For a skinny nine-year-old, he has a real loud voice. Kelly crossed her eyes at me.

Momma kissed us good night.

"I'll see you in the morning," she said. "Now, you remember what I told you. You are responsible." Then she got into the car with Aunt Nell and drove away, leaving us with Craig.

He stood in the doorway, his feet apart, arms arched at his sides, his gun tucked into the elastic of his pajamas. I could see he had on a necklace of dirt beads and crunched-up leaves with a couple of small sticks hanging from his shirt. He wiped the back of one hand across his mouth where chocolate ice cream left a brown, sticky mustache.

"Come over here and sit with us," I said.

He came over and stood between us. Craig is the only person I know who can stand in the middle and block the TV on both sides. Kelly and I have talked about it a lot, and we can't figure out how in the world he does it, him being so skinny and all.

"I'm going to be with the FBI when I grow up," he said. "And catch outlaws and murderers and killers and put them in jail and get my name and my picture in the paper. A gen-u-wine he-ro."

"Oh?" Kelly said, then she looked over at me. "After the werewolf movie there's both the old version and the new version of *The Blob*."

"Oh, boy!" I said. "Momma left us some snacks. We can eat them all in here while we watch TV."

"And when I get to be twelve, my daddy's gonna teach me to shoot a real gun. . . ."

"Yeah," Kelly said.

"But we'll have to be real careful about spilling anything, or Momma will jerk a knot in our heads."

"Your daddy got a gun?" Craig was looking down at Kelly with his eyes squinched up.

"I think she bought Fig Newtons special for tonight. Man, do I love Fig Newtons."

"I know your daddy's got a gun. Where's he keep it hid?"

"And there's some potato chips too. Papa won't tell on us if we eat in here."

"Naw, he'll eat with us."

"Yup. Your daddy keeps that gun right up next to his bed in the nightstand. I think I'll take a look at it."

"We don't touch that gun," I said, staring hard at Craig. Then we all went in the kitchen to get the snacks ready for movie time.

When Papa came home, the sun was just starting to set, and Craig had shot everything that moved and everything that didn't. He tried three times to get upstairs so he could get a good look at a real gun. When Papa walked in, we were fixin' to watch Lon Chaney. All the lights were out and the three of us were huddled on the sofa, anxious to get scared to death.

"What's this you're watching?" Papa said.

"Shhh, Papa," Kelly said. "It's a scary show."

"Yeah," I said. "About werewolves ripping people's guts out."

"Hey," Papa said. "That's old Lon Chaney. They don't make movies like they used to." And he sat down on the sofa and grabbed a handful of potato chips.

"I got my gun right here, Papa," Craig said.

"Gimme some of those cookies," Papa said, reaching for the Fig Newtons.

After a few minutes Papa said, "You mean that old Lon turns into a wolf and kills people? Now, why in the world does he do that?"

"Because a werewolf bit him one time and he didn't die," Kelly said. She was stuffing potato chips into her mouth.

"Papa, you know this story better than anybody," I said. Papa winked at me. "Save me some of those," I said to Kelly, pulling the bag away from her.

"Now for the rest of his life he has to kill people every full moon on account he turns into a wild killer beast and tears off people's arms and legs and all." Now Kelly was eating all the animal crackers.

"He knows all about this," I said. "Don't eat all those too. I want some."

"The only thing that can kill him is a silver bullet," Craig said, patting his gun.

"Hold on one second," Papa said. Now he was hogging the Fig Newtons. He always hogs the Fig Newtons. That's why Kelly and I had had to make ourselves near about sick trying to eat as many as we could hold before he got home. Daddy thinks Papa is going through his second childhood. Momma says no, he's just living his life to the fullest.

"You mean to tell me that every time the moon is

full, that wolfman comes out and kills people?" Papa said.

"Oh, Papa," I said. "You know that. I'll bet you've seen this show one million times."

"Shhh," Craig said. "It ain't as scary when you talk."

"I can't hardly hear," I said, and got off the sofa and turned the volume up. "Scoot over," I said to Kelly when I got back.

"Uh-uh," she said. "I better sit next to Papa. He might get scared." She was clutching at his arm so tight that her fingertips were starting to turn white.

"I don't remember this movie being this scary last time," Craig said.

"It's always this scary," I said.

Kelly had turned Papa loose and was sitting scrunched up, her arms wrapped around her legs.

Right in one of the very best parts, when the music was getting all scary and you just knew that the werewolf was getting ready to tear out somebody's guts, Papa hollered out, "Boo!"

"Aaaaaaaghhhhh!" Craig leaped to his feet, dancing on Momma's new sofa and grabbing for his gun.

"Haw-haw!" Papa said. He was laughing so hard, he could barely sit up.

"Don't you never do that again, Papa," Kelly said. I thought for sure she was going to start crying. "Don't you never, never do that again."

"Papa, that even scared me," I said. He just laughed.

By the end of the movie Papa had scared us three more times. Kelly was crying real quiet-like, and Craig had wet his pants all over Momma's new sofa because he was scared to go to the bathroom alone. He was wearing a pair of Kelly's underwear, and every time Papa looked at him in those frilly underpants or looked at Kelly sniffing and all bunched up, he started laughing again. Momma was going to kill us when she saw the spot on the sofa, because Kelly and I were responsible.

We could only watch part of *The Blob.*

"What?" Papa said, wiping tears from his eyes. "You're not going to watch the rest of this action-packed thriller? Are you sure you don't want to?"

"We're sure, Papa." Even my voice was shaky, and I have to be scared to get like that. Of course, Kelly and Craig are a different story. You can just about scare them to death by saying boo. So I wasn't surprised to see that they were crying and quaking. I started wishing that Momma would come home early.

"You kids really think you need all the lights in the house on?" Papa said. Then he got real quiet and serious. "I didn't want to tell you all this, but on the way home I noticed that the moon was full." He paused. "Well," he said, slapping at his legs. "I gotta run down to the VFW. Be back in a few minutes."

"No, Papa!" Kelly said. "You can't leave us alone."

I was standing at the window, peeking through the curtains at the full moon. It was huge, pasted in the sky and shining yellow and bright, aiming right at our house. A path for any werewolf to follow. My heavy breathing made a circle of steam on the glass.

"I left my hat over yonder, while I was playing cards," Papa said. "I got to go get it."

"Papa, you never wore your hat today," I said. I was expecting any minute for the head of a werewolf to show up black against the moon, the way they always do in the movies. I let the curtains close.

"Believe I did," he said, clearing his throat with a growl. "While I'm gone, if any ol' werewolf creeps up here, you remember to put silver bullets in Craig's gun so you can shoot him." Papa laughed again, and walked slow toward the door, dragging one leg behind him the way the werewolf had done. He clutched his leg like he'd been shot and looked over his shoulder the way the real wolfman did in the movie, to see if the townspeople were following to come kill him.

"Papa," I said. "You have got to stop that." I

could see that Kelly and Craig were upset, and I was feeling a little scared myself.

"By the way," Papa said, as he opened the door. "If I was you, I would turn off some of these lights—because if there was to be a real werewolf out there"—Papa paused—"he wouldn't have any trouble finding you in here."

"Please don't go," Kelly said. "Papa, please don't go. Give us a chance to turn off those upstairs lights first."

Me and Craig followed her. He had his gun drawn at his side. I went into the kitchen and searched for a flashlight. I could only find one battery.

"There were so many lights on, it looked like the house was afire," Papa said when we got back. And when he saw the flashlight, he said he thought that was a good idea. "If that wolfman was to come in here, you could beat him off with that," he said, pointing. "Or shine the light in his eyes and blind him. I wonder why nobody never thinks of that in the movies?"

Well, I didn't think that was funny.

Papa limped out the door, still holding his leg, and got to the middle of the road. Then he threw his head back and howled twice at the moon. I didn't think that was funny either.

I slammed the door hard and locked it.

"No need to worry," I said. "Because there is no such thing as werewolves."

"Where do we hide, Leah?" Kelly said.

"Under Momma and Daddy's bed," I said.

We had just gotten settled, all three of us squished under the bed, when the phone started to ring.

"Go answer it, Kelly," I said. "We'll save your place under the bed."

"What?" she screeched. "I can't go down there alone. I could get killed. Or worse."

"I'll go with you, then," I said.

"I'm not staying here by myself," Craig said.

We scooted to the end of the bed and pulled ourselves out.

"Hurry," I said. "Before it stops ringing. It could be Momma."

Kelly reached the phone first. She's faster than we are because she had track and field last year in school. Her fourth-grade teacher, Miss Beck, said she was about as fleet of foot as anybody in town. It comes in handy, I guess.

"Hello?" Kelly said. "Hello?" Then she turned to us and said, "There's nothing on here but breathing." And she went to hang up the receiver. That's when we heard the howl of the werewolf. Scared Kelly so bad, she let the phone go. It banged against the wall a couple of times, then swung back and forth.

Kelly looked at me, wide-eyed.

Another howl.

"Hang it up," I whispered.

"You," she said.

"I can't. My arms don't work."

Craig reached out, his hand shaking so bad, he could hardly hang on to the phone. Then we all stood in the kitchen as quiet as could be, not knowing what to do next. The phone rang again.

"Who do you think that is?" Kelly said.

"It might be Aunt Laura," Craig said. "Answer it. I hung it up."

"Craig's right—it might be Momma," I said. "Didn't she tell us she'd call and check on us?"

"I don't remember," Kelly said. "Answer it." She handed me the phone.

"Momma?" I said.

No answer.

"Momma, please be there. Please don't be a real werewolf, because we are already in a lot of trouble. Craig wet on the sofa, and my arms won't hardly work anymore."

There was silence and then a growl that changed into a long howl.

I can't answer that phone anymore, I wanted to say, but I was too scared for my mouth to work either. I hung up the phone.

"If that werewolf knows our phone number, does that mean he knows our address too?" Kelly said.

"Turn out the light and help me move this sofa in front of the door," I said. "If that werewolf comes in here, he won't think to turn on a light, and he'll fall over the furniture."

It took a few minutes to move the sofa. Momma says that you can always tell a good piece of furniture by how much it weighs. This one must have been worth a fortune. It was so heavy, it scratched deep marks into the wood floor. I only worried for a second about all the hours Momma and Daddy had spent refinishing the floors. I figured a few scratch marks would be okay if they saved our lives.

We went back upstairs and hid under the bed. The yellow comforter hung around the edges of the bed, nearly touching the floor. We hadn't hardly got settled again when we heard the door handle shaking, and we knew he had come for us.

Kelly screamed loud and shrill. My little scream was pretty weak compared to hers. Craig sounded like he was gargling.

"We got to be quiet," I said. "If we don't be quiet, he'll be able to find us."

"The gun," Craig said. "Get your daddy's gun." And before I could answer, he rolled from under the bed. I heard the drawer slide open and shut again.

"Here," he said, poking me in the side with it.

"Hey, don't give it to me," I said. "*You* keep it. It's your daddy teaching *you* to shoot, not mine."

"Not until I'm twelve," he said. "That's three more years." He poked me again, hard in the ribs. His voice was whiny. "Now I'll never get to join the

FBI and catch killers and robbers and get my picture in the paper."

"Oh, you'll get your picture in the paper, all right," I said. "Only nobody will know which part is you and which part is us when that werewolf gets through. And be careful with that gun, or that werewolf won't have to kill me."

Downstairs there was a loud scraping noise and then a bump. A howl split the air, and the hair on the back of my neck stood straight up. Kelly was sobbing, both of her hands over her mouth so as not to make any noise. Her elbow was digging into my neck and her knee was in my side, but I didn't even care.

"He's in," Craig said, and he started to cry. "Here, take this gun," he said in a high voice, and he put the gun on my stomach.

I had never touched Daddy's gun before. That was the rule. If we were to touch it, he would blister us, and I knew that. So I was surprised at how heavy it felt. I held the gun with both hands and pointed it in the direction I thought the door was.

"We don't have any silver bullets," Kelly said.

That's when we heard the breathing. It was loud and raspy and it was getting closer. There was a dragging noise, and I realized that the werewolf was probably hurt bad, and that would make him even meaner. I decided not to mention that to Kelly and Craig.

Could have sprained his ankle running from the mobs, I thought.

The breathing got closer, and even though I was nearly frozen with fear, I broke out sweating. Kelly was crying out loud now, and so was Craig.

"No silver bullets," she said again.

"Shhh!" I said. "He'll hear us sure."

"It don't matter," Craig said. "He can smell us."

"AAARRRRRGGGGHHHH!" the werewolf said.

Sweat trickled down my forehead, and ran toward my ears. I began to cry too.

I aimed the gun.

"AAAARRRRRGGGGHHHH!"

"Shoot him! Shoot him!" Craig screamed.

"I can't! I don't know how!" And then the gun started shooting, and it couldn't have been me, because I have never even had ahold of a gun before, much less shot one.

"I'll be cat-kicked," Papa said softly from the door. "I will be cat-kicked."

He grabbed us by the feet and pulled us from under the bed, one by one.

Papa's face was pure white in the full moon.

Momma didn't like it when she got home and saw us all awake at midnight, shaking in the kitchen. She really didn't like it when she saw the wet stain on her new sofa and it sitting whopper-jawed next to the front door, with all those scratch marks on the floor. And when she went upstairs and saw the bullet holes Papa made me shoot through her and Daddy's bed and into the ceiling, she liked that even less.

There wasn't even a word that could describe the trouble we were in. I got it good for messing with Daddy's gun. He didn't care that I was doing the best I could to protect family and self. I wasn't just on restriction till school started, but I got a hard spanking, even though Daddy said he had thought I was too old to get one. And if that wasn't enough, we had to pay out of our savings to have the ceiling fixed.

But Papa got it the worst of all. Daddy hollered that Papa was gonna have to go into an old folks home if things didn't change. Momma calmed him down, and later, after every one had either gone home or gone to bed, Kelly, Papa, and I made a pact that we would be good together until the day we died.

September

KELLY

Try as we might, Kelly and I couldn't keep the summer from ending. It made me kind of sad to think that the weather would cool off and things wouldn't be green anymore.

On the first day of school Momma was up early to fix us breakfast. She doesn't do that in the summer because she says she doesn't want us getting fat and sassy. But it's important to her that we do good in our classes, so Momma is up early every day of the school year to cook us a nutritious breakfast.

"Momma?" Kelly said. She was tying her shoes at the table, one shoe propped up on the edge. Her leg was really tan. Well, that wasn't gonna last long. Not with us sitting in a schoolroom instead of playing in the sun.

"What, Kelly?" Momma asked. "Get your foot down. You know better than that."

"Okay," Kelly said. She put her foot down and finished tying her shoes. Kelly always does what Momma asks the very first time. "We've been thinking. We've been thinking that you should buy us Pop-Tarts for breakfast."

"Yeah, Momma," I said. "The kind with icing. Strawberry."

"They're just empty calories," Momma said, and flipped over an egg.

"But we need energy for school," Kelly said. "Something to build strong bones and teeth."

"That's milk," Momma said, and set two full glasses on the table. A little bit sloshed out of one glass and landed on the flowered tablecloth. The cloth drank the milk gone like it was thirsty.

I could see we weren't going to get any Pop-Tarts from Momma. I rolled my eyes at Kelly. She tossed her blond hair back from her face and then rubbed her hand slow across her forehead. Maybe Papa would get us some. We could eat them on the way to school. Or for lunch.

"I got a headache," Kelly said. I could see her freckles really good.

"You just don't wanna go to school," I said. I was thinking that there had to be some way we could get some Pop-Tarts.

"No, I'm not kidding. Momma, my head is hurting."

"You're hungry," Momma said. "Breakfast is almost ready."

Kelly grabbed at my hand. She looked at me funny. Her face was white and she was sweating.

"Leah!" she said.

"What?" I said, and I was screaming without mcaning to. "What?"

Kelly's grip tightened. Her other hand grabbed my shirt.

"Momma!" I said. The look on Kelly's face scared me. "Momma! Help! What is it? What is it?" My voice was loud and shrill. It didn't sound like me. "Momma." The word echoed in my brain and jumbled my thoughts around.

Kelly fell out of her chair, pulling me down with her. The cushion slid toward the dining-room rug. I heard my new school shirt tear. Kelly was shaking, out of control shaking. It was like nothing I had ever seen before. Momma knelt beside us for a second, then jumped up to call for help. I could smell the eggs burning. I thought I heard a siren scream and wail, then I realized it was me.

It seemed like forever before the ambulance arrived.

"Help her, God. Help her, God," I said over and over again, even though I knew it was too late.

Without warning, Kelly died. She was there and fine one day, then dead the next. And I hadn't even known she was sick.

Dr. Cowley said they would do an autopsy, her being so young and all. Momma and Daddy didn't even answer. We were all standing together in the hall of the hospital, except for Papa, because we hadn't been able to find him. Something was making my nose itch. I think it might have been the way the hospital smelled. Clean and sick at the same time. The lights made everyone look green.

Okay, I said in my head, because no one was answering. *Just as long as you can bring my friend back.* But only the words "my friend" came. They seemed to croak out of my mouth. I couldn't control myself. It was like I was floating above the whole scene of things, unable to step in and change anything, not even myself. In slow motion Momma turned and grabbed me up close to her. Everything was so different. So different.

A pain came up in my throat.

"Ouch," I said, and started crying.

We walked out to the car and drove home. Daddy was crying and praying out loud. Momma's face was buried in his armpit, and he steered with one hand.

"God," he said over and over again. "Oh, God," and it wasn't like he was cussing or anything. He was just giving up a part of himself. Momma just moaned.

At home I cried until I thought I'd never cry

again. In the warmth of the September sun I sat cold in a ray of light that streamed in through the window, mocking me. I cried hard into my pillow.

Why didn't everything stop? It should. Everything should stop because Kelly was dead. Dead without telling me she was sick. Dead without even telling me good-bye.

I wanted to throw up, like I had wanted to once before when I'd seen a rescue team pull a boy from my fifth-grade class out of the lake in the park. He'd been under the water twenty minutes, and I stood on the sand holding Kelly's hand and thinking, *Find him. Find him.* When they finally did find his body, they wrapped it in a gray blanket and took him away. Another boy from our class, who stood with us, said, "Too bad it couldn't have been his older sister. He was the nice one in the family." I walked away cold, breathing deep gulps of air to calm my queasy stomach. The sun had kept shining that day too.

I gagged in my pillow and waited for this day to end. For it to become dark. Then in the darkness I could mourn with everything, the way I should. Mourn without the sun teasing me with its brightness. Without it running golden on my arms, showing the hairs that lay smoothly.

I heard Papa come in. I could hear him crying in the sun room, calling out his dead wife's name as he staggered in, "Anna. Anna."

Then I was standing in front of him.

"Where have you been?" I screamed. For the first time I saw how old he looked. His face was old. Old from the war. Old from losing Grammy and now Kelly. Old from living.

"Ernst told me," he said. Tears ran down the tanned creases in his face. He swayed in front of me, then covered his face with his hands and sobbed.

"Where were you when we needed you?" I said. "Where were you when Kelly needed you? When I needed you?" I was shouting loud. Papa looked at me in surprise.

I heard Momma running down the stairs from the bedroom, where she and Daddy had been. She was calling Papa's name. She sounded very far away and floaty to me.

"You old man," I screamed. "You should have been here. You should have stopped it from happening. You should have stopped it."

"I couldn't," Papa said. "I couldn't stop none of it."

"I thought you could do anything," I yelled. *"You* should be dead. Not her. She was young. She was young, and you're just an old man who gets into too much trouble, taking everyone with him. You let Grammy die and now Kelly, when you should have been the one to go. I want my sister back." I pushed Papa hard. He stumbled backward into Daddy's favorite reading chair and then onto the floor. The brass lamp toppled toward the floor, but Papa caught it before it could hit. He sat with it in his lap, looking at me with eyes that looked amazingly like Kelly's.

"You die," I screamed. "You die." Then I ran. I ran past Mrs. Comer, who was standing in her front yard, watering her roses and crying. I wondered how she knew so soon. Had she peeked in on that too? A garbled noise escaped me. I kept running. I ran all the way to Aunt Fay and Sam's house, never stopping once. I slipped into their yard and climbed into the tree house and waited.

I lay on the mattress, gasping for breath. I heard Samantha saying, "No. No." But I never got up. I heard Aunt Fay crying with her daughter. They got into their car and left, I was sure, to go to my house.

My face was burning from crying and running. Time slowed until it was barely crawling. I watched as the shadows of the tree's leaves marched around the room until they were gone, and the sun slipped away.

It was nearly eleven o'clock when I came back home. There was a chill in the air. Everything reminded me of Kelly, so sharply at times that I'd say, "Ooooooh," aloud as the pain filled me to the ends of my fingers and toes. My head hurt like someone had been pulling my hair for a long time.

"Help me, Heavenly Father," I prayed. The house

was full of family. I pushed past them all, not seeing who was there, and went upstairs and climbed into Momma and Daddy's bed, because I couldn't bear going in our room. And finally I slept.

The next day they called Daddy and told him that Kelly died from an aneurysm, that a blood vessel exploded in her head. Daddy tried to reassure us that it had been quick, that she hadn't suffered much, but I could still feel the pressure of Kelly's hand on mine, and I knew that she had hurt.

Momma's sisters arranged for Kelly's funeral. They didn't want any of us to worry about something like burying my only sister. I looked hard at Aunt Carrie when she said that they would take care of funeral arrangements. She looked back at me with sad eyes. Everyone, including Papa, was gathered around the dining-room table. I could see a faint line on the tablecloth from where the milk had spilled yesterday.

People were everywhere. They kept coming and coming. All of our relatives. Family that only gathered together for reunions found their way back to our house and then to motels and hotels to wait for the funeral. I thought if I could just make it through this awful thing that was happening now, if I could just make it through Kelly's funeral, maybe I would feel all right. But I knew that wasn't true.

The day Kelly was to be buried, the sun burned hot in the sky. The air was thick with moisture. My nose was stuffed and my head was still banging from crying. I had on a horrible black-velvet dress that itched at the collar and all the seams. Everything seemed hotter than hot in that dress.

I was amazed at the number of people that knew Kelly. The funeral parlor was full to overflowing. It seemed like all of New Smyrna was there. Mrs. Comer, Tom and his daddy and his big brother and his momma. Shelly Diamond, Otis Mulligan, Rachel Cunningham, and all their families. The principal, Mr. Ferrin, Kelly's teacher from last year, Miss Beck. And Ernst, Jesse Norman, Elmo. There were so many people, I couldn't even see them all. They were standing crowded in the back and sitting cramped on all the benches. It seemed everyone had come to tell Kelly good-bye.

And right in front of all these people I was gonna have to let my sister go, and I just didn't know if I'd be able to.

At the grave Momma stood up in the middle of the preacher's talking. She called up Aunt Fay, Aunt Carrie, and Aunt Nell. Together they sang about how merciful Jesus is and about a green hill far away. They sang a song Aunt Carrie had written for Momma when Kelly was born. Tears ran down

Momma's face, and once she sagged nearly to the ground, but her sisters held her up so that she stood tall. In all my life I never heard my mother or aunts sing better than they did that day. Or more sad.

Daddy stood up then and talked about Kelly. He told how surprised he and Momma were when three months after their first child was born, they found out they would be having another baby. He told how wonderful Kelly was. How they had loved her. How they loved her still. And how she had loved us.

I began to cry again. I could hear my aunts crying. And Samantha and Craig. It seemed like everyone was losing their friend. I cried all the hurt out of my throat, but somehow it wasn't enough.

"Hush, hush," Momma said to me.

"I can't help it," I said.

And then we were led away so they could put Kelly's body into the ground.

I couldn't go to school. The thought of being there without Kelly made my heart hurt. And I just didn't want to start crying at school, because I might not stop. Momma didn't push me either. A couple of times I heard her talking to Daddy, telling him I had to have a chance to work things out. Even though I never told her, I was thankful about that.

One night, about two months after Kelly's funeral,

when Daddy was working late, me and Momma sat watching TV. Actually I wasn't seeing anything, I just didn't want to be alone. Suddenly Momma started talking.

"When she was born, Kelly was as bald as she could be. Not you. You had a headful of hair. So much that all my sisters were always playing with it. Like you were a doll or something. It took a whole year before Kelly finally got any." We talked about Kelly for two hours till Daddy came home. When he walked in, me and Momma were laughing so hard, the tears were running down our faces. Daddy sat with us and we talked some more.

"So they weren't Kelly's ideas, all that stuff," I said, confessing the summer's adventures. "She just went along with me, because she was my friend."

I sat quietly for a minute.

"You know . . . we were so close. We could finish each other's sentences. We could read each other's thoughts." I paused because my throat was closing up tight. "I just wish I could have known. I wish I could have helped her."

It was quiet, then Momma cleared her throat. I could see her laughing tears had turned to crying ones. Daddy's face was wet with tears too.

"I just wish I had gotten her those darn Pop-Tarts," Momma said.

It made me feel better to see that Momma had regrets too. Maybe when somebody dies, there's always something you wish you had done or said or known.

"We loved her," Daddy said, "and that's what she wanted."

That night it didn't hurt quite so bad going to sleep in our room. Talking and time were making things a little bit easier.

But Papa. Papa was another story. I didn't want to talk to him. I didn't even want to see him. And try as I might, I couldn't explain the way I was feeling to Momma or Daddy. I couldn't even explain it to myself. Try as I might, I couldn't understand why seeing that Papa couldn't make things different bothered me so much. It wasn't till the night before I went back to school that Papa and I got things cleared up.

I was in my room trying to decide what I was going to wear when Papa came in. He sat down on the bed and nodded at all the things I pulled out.

"That's nice," he said about each shirt, or "That'll go real good with blue jeans." Finally, when I had looked at everything there was to look at four or five times, he said, "Why don't you and me walk on over to Wilson's for an ice-cream cone? My treat."

"Okay," I said. There was a big empty spot in my stomach remembering that Kelly wouldn't be coming along. But I didn't want to think about it.

We walked in silence for a few minutes. I had my hands stuck deep in my pants pockets.

Don't ask me to hold your hand, Papa, I thought, *because I just don't want to. I just can't.* But Papa didn't ask.

"You know," Papa said after a while, "life is not easy. And I don't think it's meant to be." His hands were stuffed in his pockets, too, and I wondered if maybe he was having a hard time like I was. "I've never told anyone this before. No one except for Grammy knows about this.

"Our first baby died. A little boy." I looked surprised at Papa. I had always thought there was just Momma and her sisters. Papa was staring off into the sky, looking past the stars.

"I never spoke about him, and I never let anyone else talk about him. It just hurt too bad. But I started thinking. And I thought aloud to your grandmother. And I came up with my ideas about what's happening here on this planet. My ideas are a lot different than those over at the church. A lot different than the preacher that's there now and the one that was there years ago when my son died. He was only three days old, and it just didn't seem right." Papa laughed, but it was a sad laugh. I hadn't heard Papa laugh really good for a long time now. "After a long time of feeling sad Grammy and I talked. We decided we couldn't always be sad. We would always love our baby, always miss him, and sometimes be angry about what had happened. But we couldn't quit living. We were lucky. We still had each other. And we could have more kids. And so we did."

We walked in silence a minute. The night sky was dark blue, almost purple, and the moon was a sad-face sliver. Up the road I could see the bright colors of Wilson's store blink off and on and off and on. I stared ahead.

"I wanna be sad and I wanna be mad," I said.

"You can," he said. "But not with me. Just don't be mad with me. I can keep on going in life if I know my last best friend is there for me. I don't want to have to do it alone."

I looked hard at Papa, thinking of all the best friends he had lost. And then it was clear to me. Clear like the night sky. Clear like the blinking light selling triple-scoop ice-cream cones. Clear and cold and scary.

"Papa," I said. "I'm afraid. If I keep on loving you, I'll lose you too. And I just couldn't stand that." I was crying. "I didn't mean what I said, Papa. I don't want you to die. I'll be all alone."

Papa hugged me close to him. I buried my face into the worn flannel of his shirt. I could feel his ribs under my fingers. I could smell the faint odor of cologne. His whiskers scratched at my cheek. We stood there hugging for a long time.

"But you got to keep loving," Papa said. I could feel my hair moving from his breath. "You can't stop loving. Then life is really tough." He squeezed me hard, pushing the air out of my lungs a little, and we started again for Wilson's. I reached for Papa's hand and held it tight.

"I want razzleberry," I said. "Can you afford a double-decker?"

"For you, Leah," Papa said, "anything."